Kestrel

Danger Bluff, Book Three

Becca Jameson

Pepper North

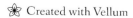

About the Book

Welcome to Danger Bluff where a mysterious billionaire brings together a hand-selected team of men at an abandoned resort in New Zealand. They each owe him a marker. And they all have something in common—a dominant shared code to nurture and protect. They will repay their debts one by one, finding love along the way.

Kestrel

A mysterious billionaire saved my life.

Now, I owe him.

My team's job: Save Zara from lurking threats.

My goal: Convince her she's mine.

Zara

I've tried to avoid attention all my life.

But there's bad guys everywhere.

Danger Bluff should be a safe place to hide...

If only that devastating pilot didn't ooze Daddy vibes.

Prologue

"Do you know what we do to murderers in here, cabrón? This ain't the Holiday Inn."

Kestrel took a step deeper into his cell but kept his shoulders back and his chin high. Bastard wasn't the worst thing he'd been called since his capture. The physical abuse was what he needed his energy to endure. He probably wouldn't survive prison in Mexico, but he sure as hell would go down fighting.

He'd been here less than two hours, and frankly, he was surprised it had taken that long for the prison gang to show up, crowding the entrance to his cell. The largest of the men, and clearly the leader, had at least fifty pounds on Kestrel. Most of it wasn't muscle, but that wouldn't matter in a fight.

Kestrel said nothing in response. He had no defense. These men were not ill-informed. Kestrel had indeed killed three men, but he'd done it for a good reason, and he would do it again in a heartbeat. No matter what happened to him, at least he knew his best friend, Stephan, and Stephan's Little, Teresa, were now safely back in the U.S.

These gang members might not tolerate murderers, but they could go fuck themselves. Kestrel didn't tolerate human trafficking, especially when it involved his best friend's girl.

Three imposing men entered the cell, fists flexing, eyes narrowed.

Kestrel had expected to meet with resistance. Hell, he'd presumed he'd be dead before the end of the month, but he hadn't thought his blood would be spilled in less than an afternoon.

"Out!" shouted someone behind the gang members. "All of you. Out now."

Kestrel had never been more relieved to have taken four years of high school Spanish.

The leader growled as he turned to face the newcomer. "We're just introducing ourselves to the new boy, guard."

"Well, you can go find something else to do. He's been transferred."

Kestrel's heart raced at this news. Transferred? Where? Why?

The men scowled at Kestrel before they slowly left his cell.

"Let's go, Galison. You've been moved." The guard looked bored as he stood at the entrance to the cell, waiting impatiently.

Kestrel took a deep breath and a step forward. He didn't need to look around. He didn't have any belongings. He hadn't even lowered himself to sitting on his bed yet.

He had no idea what this transfer was all about. No one had mentioned it to him, especially not the shitty lawyer who'd "defended" him.

"Where am I going?" he asked the guard as he followed the man, retracing his steps to the entrance.

"Fuck if I know, asshole. I'm just doing my job." The guard didn't look at him. "Hell, probably."

Of that, Kestrel had no doubt. He was already there. Wherever he was going next couldn't be worse, considering he'd been about five minutes from death before this guard had shown up.

Fifteen minutes later, Kestrel was in shackles for the second time that day and stuffed in the back of a truck. He was also alone. Fear climbed up his spine as the driver and another prison guard of some sort pulled away from the curb.

Sweat ran down his back. It was fucking hotter than hell, and there was no AC in the back of this vehicle. No ventilation either. If they went very far, he might die before they arrived, which could be a blessing.

He figured about fifteen minutes had passed when the truck suddenly veered off the road so hard that Kestrel was thrown to the floor. Thank God his hands were cuffed in front to break his fall, or he might have hit his head.

Gunfire erupted seconds later.

"What the f—" the driver shouted before he slumped over the steering wheel.

Kestrel's eyes widened in fear. The man in the passenger seat had also slumped against the door. Dead. Both of them.

"Jesus, fuck," Kestrel murmured. Whoever had ambushed them had probably done so to either kidnap or murder Kestrel. Probably both. He'd killed three human traffickers, after all. The man in charge of that crime ring probably wanted revenge.

When the back door swung open, Kestrel braced himself for death for the second time in an hour.

Four men stood outside the back of the truck. Three of them were guarding the fourth, facing the surrounding area, weapons lifted.

"Kestrel Galison?" the fourth man asked.

Kestrel swallowed. It wasn't as if he could get away with lying. This guy knew exactly who he was. And then an important detail filtered into his mind. The man was Caucasian. He spoke perfect English. And the camouflage he wore wasn't anything Kestrel had seen in Mexico.

Kestrel cleared his throat. For the first time in weeks, he had some hope. "That's me."

"Let's go. Hurry." He waved Kestrel out of the back of the truck as he turned toward one of the other men. "Spidey, grab the keys for these shackles from the guard."

One of the men nodded and jogged toward the front of the truck while Kestrel slid to the end of the vehicle and hopped awkwardly to the ground. A glance around told him they were in the middle of nowhere. The only thing he could see besides dirt in any direction was the van these men must have used to run the prison guards off the road.

The guy named Spidey returned just as fast and bent down to unlock Kestrel's ankles before doing the same to his wrists.

"Good. Let's go. Get in the van." The man in charge ushered Kestrel to the van's sliding door while the other three men continued to scan the area. These men were well-trained by some branch of the military, though they weren't with the U.S. armed forces now. Still, they were definitely former military. Same as Kestrel.

Kestrel jumped into the van and slid across the seat. Two seconds later, all four men were inside as well. Spidey slapped the dash. "Go."

The man in charge drove. One of the guys who'd taken the third row of seats tossed jeans and a T-shirt over the seat. "Change. Hurry. We don't have much time."

Kestrel quickly kicked off his shoes and shrugged out of

his khaki sweatpants and T-shirt. He lifted his ass to pull the jeans on and then donned the navy T-shirt. "Where are we going? Who are you?"

The van was moving fast. Damn fast. It also pulled off the main road in minutes. The guy sitting next to him slid the door open before turning toward Kestrel and handing him a strange gold coin. It wasn't any type of currency. It was too large and didn't have a denomination or a country imprinted on it—just a swirly design.

"It's your lucky day. You've been rescued. You'll repay your debt when the time is right. This is your marker." The guy jumped down from the van. "Hurry."

Kestrel slid out after him, confused, dumbfounded, shocked. A helicopter sat twenty yards away in the dirt. The pilot started it up at that moment, kicking dust up around them and making Kestrel cover his eyes.

"Good luck," said his strange rescuer as he climbed back into the van.

The van sped away as Kestrel ducked his head and rushed toward the helicopter. He couldn't believe this was happening. He had no idea what the hell was going to happen next, but he wasn't going to die in a Mexican prison.

Chapter One

"*Mamá...*" Zara Lynch de Flores paced back and forth in her bedroom, hands on her hips from anger she wasn't used to flaring. "This is a horrible idea."

"This is the *only* feasible option, *mija*."

Despite her irritation, her mother's endearment made her smile. The blend of the Spanish words for "my" and "daughter" demonstrated the close bond between the two. Her mother scurried toward the closet, pulled out a suitcase, and tossed it on the bed. "You're leaving for New Zealand tomorrow morning. Let's get you packed."

Zara sighed. "What if I don't want to go to New Zealand? That's on the other side of the earth." Born to an American mother and a Mexican father, Zara had spent all twenty-two years of her life shuttling back and forth between the U.S. and Mexico. She hadn't been to any other countries.

Her father was wealthy. He owned his own textile company. Her mother had a business degree and also worked for the company. Zara had grown up playing and helping in the factory and knew all the processes like the back of her hand. She'd never questioned continuing to live with her parents in their gated home. They were her everything, and Zara had never wanted for anything.

There was just one problem. She had been born cursed with all her mother's and father's best features. If she had a peso for every time someone had stopped on the street and stared at her before telling her how pretty she was, she could buy a small island. She'd learned quickly to always look down when she walked to hide her features.

"I don't like this any more than you do, *mija*, but your safety is the most important thing. Your father will do everything in his power to put an end to this threat on your life as soon as possible. In the meantime, you'll go to New Zealand, lie low, and use my maiden name only. Dropping the 'de Flores' will allow you to blend in better and give you a bit more anonymity." Even though her mother was American, she was as perfectly bilingual as Zara, and she'd called her daughter *mija* from the time she'd been born, just like any other Mexican mother.

Zara stared at her mother as the woman filled her suitcase. "To do what? Where will I be staying?"

"It's a resort. It's called Danger Bluff."

Zara chuckled sardonically. "A resort? How on earth will I be safe there? You sound like you want me to go on a long vacation. That's not my style, *Mamá*. I just finished my studies at the university. I want to get a job, not go on vacation."

"One of your father's oldest friends owns the resort, *mija*. You'll be safe there. He guarantees it. I know you had your heart set on starting your career, and you can still do that. It's just on hold. Temporarily. I promise."

Zara continued to stand in her spot, watching her mother pack, not interested in helping. She didn't really care what was put in that suitcase. She'd never been a fussy, high-maintenance kind of girl. She still wasn't as a woman. She never wore makeup and rarely wore nice clothes or bothered to do anything fancy to her hair.

She'd learned from a young age that she'd give anything to be ordinary instead of having people stare at her. So she'd let her hair fall in her face, worn a ballcap, and pretended to be a tomboy. She'd worn loose clothing, jeans, unflattering shirts, and scuffed tennis shoes.

None of that had helped. People had noticed her anyway. She couldn't avoid it. As soon as she looked anyone in the eye, they gasped. Apparently, her features were coveted—stunning blue eyes, golden brown skin, and long wavy brown hair.

Zara had even gone through a phase where she'd worn brown contacts and kept her hair in a bun, but she'd never gotten used to the contacts, and the band around her heavy hair had given her a constant headache.

So, she'd lived with her curse.

"Consider it a nice vacation," her mother insisted.

Zara groaned. "Have you ever known me to lounge by the pool, sipping cold drinks with umbrellas in them, *Mamá?*"

Her mother chuckled. "No, my studious child, but you can start now."

"Not a chance." Zara put her hands on her hips again and stood taller. It wasn't a stance she often took since it drew attention to her cursed, perfect frame. Besides her face, she was five-nine with coveted curves and high, round breasts. "I'll go under one condition."

Her mother gave an exasperated sigh. "What, *mija?*"

"That I have to take a job, working for the resort."

Chapter Two

Kestrel controlled his rock-steady hand from shaking with iron determination as he held the jump drive in his palm. It contained his assignment, and everyone around the dinner table knew it.

Sadie, Rocco's Little girl, had just handed him the envelope containing the jump drive. Celeste was the only other woman in their group so far. She was sitting on her Daddy's lap, waiting as anxiously as the rest of them. Hawking had his arms wrapped around her, holding her. The rest of the team —Magnus, Phoenix, and Caesar—were currently breathing out sighs of relief that they hadn't been the one to receive this next assignment.

It wasn't that any of them minded being assigned to protect another person with their life, but they hadn't even had a chance to catch their collective breaths after a trip across the ocean to put an end to the threat to Celeste's life.

Kestrel knew the drill. All six men on this team were former military, trained to save lives at the risk of their own.

Kestrel had been in the Air Force for several years in his twenties. He was a pilot. He prided himself on being able to fly just about anything he climbed into. Currently, his official job at Danger Bluff Mountain Resort was a cushy one—taking guests on helicopter tours.

All of them had jobs at the resort, and though they did them every day of the week, the truth was those occupations were a front for what they'd been hired to do: save lives. Their benefactor—Baldwin Kingsley III—was the man in charge. He was mysterious, and none of them had met him. They didn't even know where he lived on this planet. However, they owed him, and when he gave them their assignments, they accepted the jobs and went to work.

Adjusting his ballcap further over his eyes, Magnus pushed from the table and stood. "I assume you'd like me to open that jump drive before we dive into dinner."

Phoenix chuckled. "Hell, it's not my assignment, and even I want to see the information before we eat."

All eight of them moved to hover around the computer center as Magnus slid the jump drive in and pulled up the details.

Kestrel lowered himself onto the chair next to him to get the best view.

Magnus started reading off the details. "Zara Lynch. Mother's American. Father's Mexican. Wealthy. Educated. Twenty-two years old. And... My God."

Kestrel's breath hitched as he read ahead. "She's in the sights of a human trafficking ring," he murmured. "Fuck." A shudder wracked his body. If there was one thing he abhorred more than anything in the world, it was human trafficking, and he'd certainly had his fair share of dealing with it in the past. It was why he'd landed in a Mexican prison, after all.

"Why?" Celeste asked. "Revenge or something?"

Magnus scrolled slowly through the information until he came to several photos of her.

Kestrel stopped breathing. So did everyone else.

The woman in the photos was stunning. Granted, they'd thought the same thing about Celeste and Sadie when they'd met those two, but Zara was... There were no words to describe how gorgeous she was.

"I see why," Magnus muttered.

Kestrel's hackles rose for no good reason. He considered punching Magnus's shoulder for ogling his girl.

My girl? What the hell was he thinking? She was no more his girl than anyone else's. He didn't have a claim on her. Just because Rocco and Hawking had found their perfect Little girl during their assignments didn't mean the same would happen for Kestrel.

Nevertheless, he felt a strong pull toward her, and he knew none of the guys would challenge him on this. They'd joked about Kingsley having some bizarre matchmaking abilities, but so far, the man had been spot on, so it was assumed even before opening this jump drive that the woman would end up being Kestrel's perfect Little girl.

"I know her," Celeste declared, leaning in closer. "I mean, I don't *know* her, know her. I mean, I've seen her before. She's been featured in a few magazines as one of the world's most beautiful humans. Each time, it was noted that she didn't choose to give an interview to accompany the photos."

Sadie gasped and leaned between everyone to get a better look. "I know her, too. We all do. Kingsley sent me her resume, and I hired her. She's been working here at Danger Bluff in housekeeping for a week."

Kestrel jerked his gaze to Sadie. "Are you serious? How could I have not seen her before?" It seemed impossible. If he'd seen this woman at any point in his life, he would have remembered it.

Hawking responded. "We've been beyond busy lately, Kestrel, focusing on wrapping up our last mission." He pulled Celeste into his arms and held her protectively.

"Plus," Sadie added, "now that I think of it, Zara hides her looks at all times. I've never seen her without a ballcap pulled down over her eyes. She lets her hair conceal her face, wears baggy clothes, and rarely speaks to anyone. I just assumed she was shy or introverted."

Kestrel didn't even have to ask Magnus to start panning through every camera inside and outside the resort's main building. Magnus was sharp and on it, already scanning through the many monitors spread out in front of them.

After a few seconds, Kestrel spotted her. He pointed toward one of the monitors on the right. "There she is. Why is she still working at this hour of the evening? It's after six." He glanced at Sadie. "What are her hours?"

Sadie winced. "I don't know why she's working. Her hours are six AM to two. No one likes that shift, and she said she'd prefer it, so she took it. She starts in the laundry room in the early morning, getting all the carts ready for the rest of the staff to clean rooms."

Kestrel leaned in closer. Zara was in the laundry room now. She was folding towels, concentrating hard to get them each perfect. When she didn't like one, she redid it. The night manager in the laundry came up to her while Kestrel stared at them and tapped his watch. When Zara shook her head, the man rolled his eyes and walked away.

"I'm sorry," Sadie murmured. "I didn't realize she works more than her assigned hours. I'll talk to her tomorrow."

Kestrel pushed to standing. "Nope. *I'll* talk to her tomorrow. She's my assignment." He had no idea what he would say, but he'd be in the laundry room before the sun came up in the morning, starting his assignment.

Chapter Three

"Zara... I told you not to come in this morning." The firm voice came from Mark, the man in charge of the laundry room.

Zara slid right by him with a stack of perfectly folded sheets. She shrugged, hoping he would leave her be if she just kept working.

He didn't. He followed her. "Zara, it's five-thirty in the morning. And that would be fine if you hadn't been here working until eight o'clock last night. You may only work eight hours a day, five days a week. Those are the rules."

She shrugged as she put the sheets on the shelf. "I couldn't sleep."

"Then you need a hobby or to sign up for one of the excursions or go shopping in town. You can't work sixteen hours a day." He stood firm, hands on his hips, feet planted. He even gave her his deepest scowl, though she knew inside he was a softy, so it was hard for him to pull off an effective reprimand.

"I can work as many hours as I want, Mark. I can only get

paid for eight hours a day, but if I like to spend my free time folding laundry, who's going to stop me?"

"I am."

At the sound of the new voice behind her, Zara spun around so fast she nearly tripped over her own feet and fell.

The newcomer stood at the entrance to the laundry room. He also had his hands on his hips, trying to look formidable and imposing, just like Mark. She didn't know who he was, and for a moment, she feared maybe he'd been sent to kidnap her.

She took a step backward as irrational panic consumed her. She had no reason to believe the men who'd intended to traffic her had found her, but panic seeped under her skin every time she met someone new.

The man was tall. At least six-four. He was also incredibly handsome, even with the reprimanding look on his face. The look that disappeared immediately when she collided with Mark as she stumbled into him.

The newcomer's face softened instantly as he rushed forward and took her arm, steadying her. "Are you okay?"

She pulled herself together and eased her arm out of his grip. "I'm fine." She glanced at his polo shirt and realized it had the Danger Bluff resort logo on the front. In addition, he wore a nametag. *Kestrel Galison.*

He works here, too. Get a grip.

"What's this about you working too many hours?" he asked, his voice gentle and kind.

"Maybe you can talk some sense into her, Kestrel," Mark said. "This woman works her fingers to the bone, day and night. She never takes a break."

Kestrel frowned, his gaze coming to hers again. He stood so close she could smell his body wash and his personal outdoorsy scent. "Why? Do you need the extra money for something?"

She shook her head, trying to keep her mind clear. This guy was distracting in a way she didn't have time for. Something about him made her want to step closer instead of farther away. She wished he would wrap his arms around her and hold her.

Lord knew she could use some comfort. She'd been on pins and needles for the entire week since she'd arrived at this resort. She was jumpy and nervous all the time. She hadn't been kidding about not being able to sleep. How could she be expected to sleep knowing that a human trafficking ring was intent on finding her and kidnapping her?

"Zara?" he said, reminding her that he'd asked a question.

"Oh, no. I just don't like to be idle. I like to work. Are you one of the managers here? I'm not trying to make extra money or anything. You don't have to worry about that."

She hadn't met this man, but she'd heard six men basically ran the place, filling a variety of capacities. She also knew the owner was Baldwin Kingsley III, but she hadn't seen him yet. She also hadn't seen him in her entire life. She'd simply always known he was a friend of her father.

Kestrel was staring at her, and she jerked her face down immediately. She pulled her hair over her shoulders and adjusted her ballcap so it shadowed her face more. She'd gotten complacent while working in the laundry room, especially when Mark was the only other person there.

Mark had shown no signs of knowing who she was, nor had he stared at her at any point like many people did. She liked Mark. It was refreshing working for him. No pressure. Just two humans doing their job.

But this gorgeous man standing too close to her was staring. Even though she wasn't looking him in the eye anymore, she could feel his gaze on her. It was unnerving, and she shivered. "I should get back to work," she murmured as she tried to sidestep him.

"No. You shouldn't," both men said in unison.

She glanced at Mark with wide eyes. *Traitor.*

"Mark is right. You work too much," Kestrel said. "You should come have breakfast with me."

She gasped and glanced at him for a moment before tearing her gaze away again. It was hard. Usually, she had no difficulty keeping her head down and avoiding eye contact with people, but this man was intense. Mesmerizing.

He wasn't leering at her like most men did. His look didn't say, "I want to take all your clothes off and drool over you." His expression was one of concern and genuine kindness.

Did he say breakfast? As his suggestion registered, she sucked in a breath. Was he asking her on a date? Or more like demanding? Surely not.

"Uh, do you take all new employees to breakfast so you can get to know them better?" she asked.

"Nope."

She flinched. Nope? That was all he was going to say?

He took a step closer as another employee arrived, causing Mark to rush off and speak to the woman. Kestrel's voice was soft as he spoke again. "Please, Zara. Come eat breakfast with me."

"It's too early for breakfast," she pointed out. It wasn't even six, but that was a very lame excuse, and she doubted he would buy it.

He gasped dramatically. "It's never too early or too late for breakfast. Sometimes, I like eating it for lunch, dinner, or late into the night. Please don't tell me you're a breakfast hater," he teased.

She couldn't keep from smiling or glancing at him again. This time, she let her gaze linger for a moment longer. He was so striking. She felt magnetically pulled to him.

Stop it, she reprimanded herself. *He's your boss, and you have goals.* None of them involve getting into any relationship with a man. How old was he anyway? Forty? Probably not that old. Maybe early thirties.

"I don't usually eat breakfast," she argued. She absolutely could not sit down at a table with this intense man. Out of the question.

Another gasp. "Ever? Not even for dinner?"

And this time, she giggled, causing herself to slap her palm over her mouth at the sound. When was the last time she'd laughed? Or even felt joy?

He held out a hand. "Come, Little one. Please."

Her breath hitched. Little one? It was such an odd endearment, especially coming from a man she presumed to be her boss's boss. She'd never heard anyone use that sort of endearment. Not in real life. Only in books. And only in the kind of books that secretly filled her eReader. No one knew about the type of books she liked to read when she was alone.

Surely, he hadn't meant it *that* way. She'd never met anyone who actually practiced some kind of age play. She must have misunderstood or misheard him.

His hand was still extended, palm up. He was patiently waiting. "You don't need to work this morning, Zara. Come to the dining room with me. I promise I'm a good guy. The dining room is a public place. We'll eat, and you can tell me why you don't like breakfast." His teasing voice was back.

"I never said I don't like breakfast. I just meant I don't eat this early in the morning."

"Do you drink juice, milk, coffee, or tea at this hour?"

She sighed and lifted her gaze again to face this persistent man. "I could use some coffee," she admitted, kicking herself immediately. Why was she consenting to this? Sitting at a table with this man would mean she'd have to look him in the eye, and that wasn't something she did.

The only people she ever held eye contact with were her parents and a few close friends. Except she didn't really have any of those, and certainly not anymore. The few women she'd been friendly with at school had graduated, gotten jobs, and moved on. Chances were she wouldn't remain in contact with any of them.

A deep, penetrating loneliness suddenly overwhelmed her, and she pursed her lips to keep from crying. Zara was not a crier. She was strong. Determined.

Except when you're weak and pitiful.

Kestrel wiggled his fingers again—such a bossy man.

Feeling like she was inexplicably drawn to him, she set her smaller hand in his. A strange zing traveled up her body, making her shiver.

"Thank you, Zara," he whispered as he turned to lead her out of the laundry room.

She tugged her hand free before they reached the entrance, partly because the connection made her feel light-headed and partly because she couldn't walk through the resort holding her boss's hand. People would talk. The last thing she needed was to draw attention to herself.

Suddenly, she stopped walking in the middle of the hall-way. This was a terrible idea. Zara didn't like public places. Even though it was early, some guests would already be eating in the dining room. More would join them soon. People tended to stare at her in crowds. In addition, she was always paranoid. What if one or more of the guests was an imposter sent to grab her at just the right, opportune moment?

"I can't," she murmured. How was she going to get out of this?

Kestrel turned to face her. He reached out to gently cup her face with both hands, tipping her head back. "What can't you do, Little one?"

She swallowed.

"Which part makes you nervous? Having coffee with me? Or is it the dining room?"

She sucked in a breath. He was perceptive. "Both."

"You don't like public spaces, do you, Zara?"

"No, Sir." She winced inside. What made her call him Sir?

He gave her a slow smile. "So, it's not me you're opposed to. It's the dining room."

"Uhh." She certainly wasn't opposed to *him*. But she didn't want him to know that. "I'm sorry. I promise not to work so many hours. I'll just go back to my room. There's a coffee pot in there. You don't have to waste your time having a get-to-know-the-new-girl breakfast. It's fine. Really."

His hands slid back so that his thumbs were on her pulse points. He also took a step closer, invading her space in a way that made her breathe heavily. "Zara, I don't want to discuss your work schedule this morning. We can deal with that later. And I told you I have never taken another employee to breakfast. My reasons are complicated. I'd like to explain them to you over coffee or whatever else you'd like to consume. I thought perhaps you'd be more comfortable meeting with me the first time in a public spot, but I realize now that was foolish. You don't like crowds. Understandable. Can you trust me enough to go somewhere alone? We could stop by the front desk first and let Sadie or whoever is working at reception this morning know where we're going if it would give you some peace of mind. We could go to your room or mine if you'd prefer."

Her heart was beating faster and faster. She chewed on her bottom lip, trying to find a way out of this. Nothing good could come from her spending time alone with this amazingly gorgeous man. She was too attracted to him, which was causing her to get tongue-tied. Plus, she didn't have time to deal with a romantic interlude. Not with anyone.

She wasn't here in New Zealand to date men and pretend her life was normal. She was here to hide and lie low. She didn't want to explain her reasons to this man or anyone else. She hadn't told a soul at the resort why she was here. It was easier that way. She certainly didn't want anyone to look at her with pity. That would be worse than gawking at her in lust. Well, men, anyway. Men did that. Women usually sneered at her with jealousy. She wasn't sure which was worse.

"I have a better idea," Kestrel suggested before she could formulate the words to tell him this was not going to happen. "There's a conference room near reception. We'll stop by and tell the receptionist we're using the conference room. I'll order food and coffee and have the kitchen bring it to us there. Neutral ground that doesn't have the pressure of being your apartment or mine."

She released her lip. There was no way she was getting out of this. "Okay," she found herself saying in agreement.

Horrible idea, Zara. The worst in the history of ideas.

Chapter Four

Kestrel tried hard to control his breathing as he set a hand on the small of Zara's back and guided her first to the front desk, where he informed Liz where he and Zara would be meeting, and then to the conference room.

It had been challenging getting her here, and he was relieved. For a few minutes, he'd thought she would totally decline and run away. He would have let her go, of course. He couldn't exactly force her to meet with him.

He could have just told her up front why he wanted to talk to her, but he hadn't wanted to do so in public, not even in front of Mark. What he had to say really needed to be between him and Zara. No one else.

In retrospect, the conference room was a much better choice than the dining room. If she grew nervous or panicked, at least no one besides Kestrel would see her reactions.

Kestrel pulled out a chair for her and took her hand to help her settle. As soon as she was perched on the fancy rolling leather chair, she adjusted herself, spine straight and rigid, hands folded in her lap.

"This isn't a job interview, Zara," he informed her as he sat in the chair beside hers. He smiled at her, hoping to ease her nerves as he pulled out his phone. "How about I text the kitchen and have them bring us a few danishes, some fruit, and coffee?"

"Okay," she murmured.

"Do you like cream and sugar?" he asked.

"Yes, Sir. Thank you."

As soon as the text was sent, he set the phone on the large oval table and faced her. "Please relax, Zara." He knew that was asking a lot, but he hated how tense she was with him.

She nodded, but no part of her relaxed.

Damn, she was stunning. Not just beautiful. Lots of people were beautiful. That was superficial. He was attracted to her mind already. She was bright and sharp and a hard worker. He thought she might also be Little, which would be icing on the cake.

She was certainly submissive. Maybe not with everyone, but she was with him. She'd called him *Sir* twice and not in a gracious southern belle sort of way. She'd used it reverently, whether she knew it or not.

He decided it would be best just to tell her exactly what he knew. Keeping information from her would only alienate her in the long run and probably piss her off.

"I want to be blunt about a few things, Zara."

She pursed her lips, not meeting his gaze.

"Can you look at me, Little one?"

Her breath hitched as she slowly lifted her head. Her cheeks were pink. He liked the way she reacted when he called her *Little one*. He'd tested that water out and then done it a few more times when she hadn't slapped him.

"You don't like to look people in the eye, do you, Zara?"

"No, Sir."

He'd much rather she call him Daddy than Sir, but she wasn't ready to hear that yet. First things first. He was going to pile a lot on her plate and give her much to think about, but addressing the possibility she was Little was last on the list.

"I know who you are and why you're here, Little one. I've been assigned to protect you."

She gasped, her jaw dropping as her stunning blue eyes went wide. A man could get lost in those eyes. Anyone could. He suspected that was why she disliked making eye contact with people. It would get old fast having people comment about their color or stare at her.

"I'm aware that your father is a personal friend of Kingsley, and he agreed to make sure you're protected. That's my job." Kestrel leaned forward, putting his elbows on his knees while leaning closer to her. He waited as she absorbed that first bomb of information.

She licked her lips, her spine stiffening further. "I didn't know anyone knew."

"They didn't. Not until last night. That's when I found out."

"Do you think I'm in imminent danger?" Her eyes widened again.

He shook his head. "No. Nothing like that. There's no evidence to suggest anyone has any idea where you are. Kingsley arranged for all your documents to be legally expedited so you can live and work indefinitely in New Zealand." He reached out a hand and set it on top of hers in her lap. "You're safe here."

A knock at the door made him reluctantly release her to stand and go retrieve their breakfast. When he opened the door, he found one of the kitchen staff with a cart laden with options. "Thank you so much, Edmond. I'll take it from here." He wanted to excuse the young man, so Zara wouldn't have to face him.

Kestrel pushed the cart to their side of the room before unloading everything onto the table. He glanced at Zara several times, letting her process what he'd said. She was pale now and looked distressed. He hated that.

Kestrel poured them both a cup of coffee, added cream and sugar to hers, and slid it toward her. "Take a drink, Little one."

She glanced at the spread on the table as though she'd been unaware of its presence until this moment. She really was stressed about this situation. Was it because he knew? Because it was him? Or because she was stressed about being found in general?

Ignoring the coffee, she turned back to him. "You're misinformed if you think I'm safe."

He nodded. "I can understand why you'd feel that way, but I assure you there is no safer place on earth."

She glanced around at random. "This is a tourist resort, Kestrel. Not a fortress."

He grinned. "It's every bit a fortress as well as a resort. There's even a giant saferoom in the basement below where we're sitting right now. Besides me, five other men are living and working here for Kingsley. All of us are former military, hired to protect the innocent. We all have different strengths. Together, we're a force to be reckoned with. Security cameras are trained on every inch of this property, inside and out. Few places in the world are safer than where you're sitting right now."

Her mouth fell open again. "I didn't know that."

He smiled. "Now you do."

"And you're like my bodyguard or something?"

He shrugged, trying to remain nonchalant. "Now that

I've met you, I'm hoping to become more to you than simply a bodyguard."

She licked her lips. "You're serious."

"Yes."

"We just met."

"We sure did, and I suspect you feel the same attraction I feel." He lifted a brow, challenging her to deny the truth. She'd given him every sign she was affected by him, from trembling when he touched her, her pinkening cheeks, and her fidgeting at his intense scrutiny.

"It doesn't matter what I feel or don't feel," she whispered, looking away. "My life is a disaster. I don't have the time or energy for a man."

He gently set his hand on top of where she had hers folded in her lap again and squeezed. "My job is to make you feel so safe that you'll be able to sleep at night and enjoy life more. That will give you more energy and time."

She shook her head. "You don't understand the level of stress I'm under. I sleep with one eye open and my clothes on, Kestrel. The reason why I prefer to work long hours is to keep my mind off my problems. I'm about forty-eight hours from snapping," she admitted.

He knew it was huge for her to divulge so much to him. He hadn't expected to fully take over her life this morning, but now that he knew more, it was the best option. "There's a spare room in my apartment on the fifth floor. We'll move you into it today. You can nap this afternoon without worrying and sleep all night, knowing you're safe." He squeezed her hands again. "I will not let anything happen to you, Little one."

"Why do you call me that?"

He smiled. "Because you responded to it the first time. Because you know exactly what I mean when I call you Little one. I'd guess you have no experience exploring that side of yourself, but I'd also bet you're intrigued and willing if the right person came along to give you the opportunity."

"And you think that's you," she stated bluntly.

"Yes, I do."

"Has anyone ever told you that you're overbearing and Dominant to the point of controlling?"

He chuckled. "A time or two, yes. Has anyone ever told you that you craved an overbearing Daddy in your life? Someone you can count on every moment of every day? Someone whose lap you could crawl onto when the world is scary? Someone you could cry on when you're sad and laugh with when you're happy?"

She sat rigid. Not blinking. Staring him in the eyes. Suddenly, two tears broke loose and slid down her cheeks.

Kestrel released her hands, dragged her chair closer, and took a risk. He lifted her off her seat and settled her sideways on his lap. He eased her ballcap off, set it on the table, and pressed a hand to the back of her head, encouraging her to rest her cheek on his shoulder.

Zara silently cried, nearly breaking his heart, but he also knew she'd probably carried around this pent-up need for release for a long time. Not just a week. Months. Perhaps years. She needed a good cry.

He reached for a few napkins from the table and handed them to her, which made her cry harder.

"Stop being nice to me," she grumbled.

He chuckled and held her tighter. She fit so perfectly on his lap, like she was meant to be right here.

When her tears finally dried to sniffles, she tipped her red-rimmed eyes back to look at him again. "How old are you?"

"Thirty-three."

She nodded slowly.

"Too old for you?" he teased.

She shrugged. "I've never really dated, so..."

His heart seized. "Why not?"

She drew in a deep breath. "Mostly because I've never been able to trust anyone to like me for me. Men ask me out—every day, even when I'm hiding under a ballcap and baggy clothes. It drives me nuts. I hate it. They don't care about my personality or what I like or don't like. They only care about my looks."

"Well, I care about your personality and your likes and dislikes. Plus, I won't even ask you out. I'll just move you into my apartment." He grinned.

She finally gave him a partial smile. "You can't do that."

"Why not?"

"It's not proper or whatever. People would talk. What if your co-workers found out? They'd think I was a floozy."

He flinched. "No one will ever think you're a floozy, Zara. I promise. I'll let you in on a secret. All six men on my team are Daddy Doms. Two of them have even found their forever Little girls. All of us live together on the fifth floor in six apartments. We're a family. When Rocco met Sadie, he moved her into his apartment. When Hawking met Celeste, he did the same with her. They'd be far more suspicious if I *didn't* move you in than if I did. They would worry about you."

She chewed on her bottom lip as she pondered his words.

He continued. "I'll tell you another secret. I haven't slept much between the time I got your assignment last night and now. I paced in the control room most of the night, watching the security cameras to be sure no one came to your door or even entered your floor."

Her eyes widened. "There aren't cameras inside my apartment, are there?"

"No. There aren't any cameras in private places. The only one on the fifth floor is at the entrance to our private quarters at the top of the stairs next to the elevator. It's only there to ensure no one comes up there snooping around."

She continued to look at him, which pleased him. At least she'd stopped glancing away.

"So, you see, we'll both sleep better if you move into my apartment."

"Because you have a second bedroom, right?"

"Yes, Little one. It's more of a playroom. It's already furnished and ready for the perfect Little girl to move in and decorate it to make it her own."

She gasped. "You're serious."

"Totally."

"A playroom," she deadpanned, looking at him as if she couldn't believe what she'd heard him say.

"Yes. A room where you can be yourself and relax at whatever age you enjoy. A room with toys and games and dolls. Coloring books, puzzles, stuffed animals. Whatever you want."

She scrunched up her face, having no idea how adorable she was. "I'm too old for toys."

He gasped dramatically. "No one is too old for toys, Little one."

"I don't think I understand what's going on here. You know that a trafficking group of slimeballs is after me. You know that I'm working here to hide. You haven't seen anyone coming after me, but you want me to move into a playroom on a private floor that is attached to your room. Does that sound as fishy to you as it does to me?" she asked, sliding off his lap again to sit in her own chair.

Kestrel controlled the corners of his mouth from smiling. She would not appreciate his amusement. He loved that Zara was intelligent and, when backed into a corner, didn't allow her natural quietness to keep her from defending herself.

"Little girl…" Kestrel said as he tried to decide how best to handle this.

A knock on the door captured his attention, and he turned around to see Sadie at the door. "Did you need this room?" he asked the front desk manager.

"No. You're fine with having the conference room this morning. I just wanted to talk to Zara," Sadie said quickly.

"Of course," Kestrel waved to invite her inside.

"I wanted to see if I should remove Zara from the schedule," Sadie asked.

"No!"

"Yes."

Zara's and Kestrel's answers came at the same time.

"I need to work. I can't just sit around," Zara said quickly.

"The laundry room isn't safe. Anyone could take advantage of the noisy machines and the isolated spot. The doors are always open to allow the heat to escape," Kestrel pointed out.

"I always close them when I'm there alone," Zara said.

"I pulled up your application. It's pretty bare," Sadie commented. "Do you have any formal education or training?"

Another voice had them all turning toward the door. "Hi! I'm checking for a shipment of supplies, and they told me Sadie was in here. Am I interrupting?" Celeste asked, coming into the conference room.

Kestrel stopped himself before he could roll his eyes in frustration. What was this? Grand Central Station, New Zealand style? His "alone time" with Zara wasn't working out very well.

"You're..." Zara pointed at the now-famous scientist.

"Hi! We haven't met. I'm..."

"Celeste Blanke. Dr. Celeste Blanke! It's an honor to meet you," Zara said, standing to offer her hand. "You're like a legend for women scientists."

"That's very kind of you to say," Celeste said with a dismissive wave.

Kestrel and the other men had been very impressed that she hadn't let the publicity and news coverage go to her head. She'd received a lot of offers when her research had hit the news waves. To her Daddy's delight, she had chosen to work from Danger Bluff.

"How do you know about Celeste?" Sadie asked with a curious look on her face.

"We studied her discoveries in my research class at the university. I just finished my last semester, and we had a great teacher who sent us out ready to conquer the world after studying Dr. Blanke's findings," Zara explained.

"Zara, call me Celeste. I'm glad to meet you, and that is very flattering. Most scientific research is mind-blowingly repetitive. Nothing ever works the first time. If I only had a research assistant here, I could do so much more. I don't suppose your research class was in scientific methods...?"

Zara nodded. "I couldn't use my degree, but I loved studying for it."

Celeste clapped her hands. "Sadie, it's official. I'm stealing your laundry assistant."

"What?" Zara said, looking back and forth between the two women.

"Of course. Take my best employee," Sadie said with a grin that took all the sting out of her words. Kestrel could tell she wasn't upset at all.

"Kestrel, will you bring her down to my workspace?" Celeste asked. "Does she know?"

"Do I know what?" Zara asked, glancing around at all of them at the same time.

"I was talking to Zara about her safety and that she would be safer to stay in the playroom attached to my apartment," Kestrel explained.

"I love my playroom," Celeste said. "Now, I sleep with D—Hawking, of course."

"You weren't going to say Daddy, were you?" Zara asked, widening her blue eyes.

"Yes. Thank goodness you guessed. It was going to be tough to keep that secret," Sadie said, jumping in.

"You have a Daddy, too?" Zara questioned in an amazed tone.

Kestrel let Sadie nod in response before saying, "I think Zara and I need to talk alone. She has a lot of things to absorb right now."

"You don't think we're weird because we have Daddies, do you?" Celeste's straightforward question caused everyone to look at Zara to judge her reaction.

"No..."

When she struggled to figure out how to answer, Kestrel came to her aid. "Zara understands Daddies and Littles. We'll talk more later. Okay?"

Sadie linked her arm with Celeste's, and the two women left the couple alone.

When it was quiet again in the conference room, Kestrel stood to walk to the door. "I'm going to lock this so we don't have anyone else come inside. You can get out easily by turning this lever."

He returned to her side and sat down. "Are you okay?"

"Overwhelmed," she admitted with a tight smile.

"May I touch you?" Kestrel asked.

"What are you going to do?"

"Just this." He lifted her onto his lap again and rocked his chair slowly, rubbing a hand over her spine. Her stiff posture softened, and she melted against his chest.

"No one is going to judge you here, Little girl. The whole team is here to keep you safe."

"You, especially?"

"Definitely."

Several minutes later, she asked, "I could sleep close to you...? For protection?"

"Yes, and I would sleep better knowing you're safe."

"Okay. I'm not agreeing to anything else," she said.

"Everything at your speed, Zara," he promised. "Would you like some food and coffee now?"

"Yes, please."

Chapter Five

Zara's mind was spinning with possibilities as Kestrel turned her slightly, angling her body on his lap so she could reach the table. He dragged her coffee closer. "You need to eat, Little one."

She picked up the mug and took a sip. It had cooled off, but not too badly.

"Cold?"

She shook her head. "No. It's just right. I don't like to burn my mouth." She took another sip, set the cup down, and eyed the danishes. "Maybe I could eat something." Suddenly, her mouth was watering. The pastries looked like they might fall apart in her mouth. The fruit also looked fresh and delicious.

Kestrel picked up a blueberry and brought it to her lips.

She hesitated but then opened her mouth and let him pop it in. It was perfectly ripe. "Mmm. Those are so good."

He offered her another.

She giggled, shocked by the sound of laughter coming from herself. "You don't have to feed me, Kestrel."

"Ah, but I enjoy feeding you. I'm going to enjoy doing lots of things for you."

"Is that in the bodyguard description? You're supposed to sit me on your lap and feed me?"

He chuckled. She loved the sound and the way it vibrated through her body. "Those things and many more are not in the bodyguard handbook. They're in the Daddy handbook."

"Mmm. And you think you're going to be my Daddy," she murmured.

"I *know* I am. But don't let me rush you. You take your time figuring it out."

"You don't want to rush me, but you want me to move in with you today?"

"Yep. Immediately. That doesn't mean I'm going to take you to my bed. I won't do something like that until you're sure you're ready."

"How chivalrous," she said sarcastically.

He shocked her when his hand lifted from around her to her waist and tickled her, making her buckle her body in that direction. "Hey!"

"Why do I get the feeling you're going to challenge me every step of the way?" He was smiling.

She shrugged. "Probably because I am. I'm a skeptical person by nature. I've had to be. From the time I was aware, I've known that most people got close to me for their own gain. I'm slow to trust. I've had very few close friends in my life, and I never trust men."

"Understandable. I will prove myself to you."

"Are you always so bossy and confident?"

"Yes. Are you always so squirmy and pink-cheeked?"

She stiffened, not looking him in the eyes as she reached for a croissant.

He wrapped a hand around hers and drew their combined hands to her lap. "Humor me," he whispered in her ear.

She shivered at his tone and the feel of his warm breath on her neck. What was he going to do now?

He managed to rip off a corner of the croissant and brought it to her lips.

She opened for him without overthinking things. The bite was delicious, but the scene was on fire. She never dreamed she'd be in a position like this. She was sitting on the lap of the most handsome man—a man she was attracted to—and he was feeding her. It was sensual and erotic. It made her feel as submissive as the heroines in her romance novels, especially the ones with Little girls and Daddies.

She didn't protest as he continued to feed her. She sat very still and opened her mouth over and over like a baby bird. Every bite tasted better because he was the one feeding her.

When she was stuffed, she shook her head and turned her mouth away. "I'm full."

He'd been feeding himself between giving her bites, and he popped that last one in his mouth, chewed, and swallowed before bringing his lips to her ear again and whispering, "I can't wait for you to call me Daddy."

She trembled in his arms as he wrapped them around her and held her close.

Zara felt like she had stepped into another dimension. She was outside of her body, living in a romance novel. This couldn't be real. She also hadn't thought about the human traffickers hunting her for over an hour. She hadn't gone that long without letting panic seep in for weeks.

She needed to extricate herself from this situation before

she said or did something embarrassing. "I should get to work."

Kestrel picked up his phone, tapped the screen, and stared at her until someone answered. "Mark, it's Kestrel. Zara is going to change positions. Will that cause you problems today?"

Kestrel held the phone between them on speaker. "Goodness, no. She did so much work yesterday that we have more than enough towels and sheets to restock the rooms today. The only thing she'd probably do would be to refold everything because she's a perfectionist," he said with a chuckle.

"Perfect."

"Will you let her know I'm going to miss her? She was the best employee I've had. But I had a feeling she wouldn't stay in the laundry room long. I'll look forward to seeing her around the resort."

"I'll let her know, Mark. Thanks. Sorry to snarl up your workload."

"No problem. We're flexible. Have a great day." Mark ended the call.

Zara glared at Kestrel. "Shouldn't I have made sure Celeste is okay with my skills before I quit my job?"

"You saw her reaction. She's ecstatic. Besides, you said yourself that I'm sort of your boss, so I can and I did make this change. You've been working too many hours. I insist you take today off. We'll move your things to my apartment and order more things for your playroom. After that, I'll take you to the basement to talk to Celeste and meet Magnus. Magnus is our computer genius. He mostly hides out in the basement monitoring things."

She wasn't sure whether to hug him or argue some more. "But..." But what? He wasn't wrong. She had worked too many hours, and he was offering her the world. He'd also shown no signs that he was being nice to her simply because she was pretty.

Granted, some people could hide their ulterior motives. She narrowed her gaze and challenged him. "You said you read about me last night. You saw pictures, too. Are you doing all this because you think I'm pretty?"

"Nope. I won't deny you are indeed the most gorgeous woman I've ever seen." He tapped her nose. "You can't hide it even under a ballcap. However, I'm doing all this because I can feel a connection with you already that tells my heart you're the perfect Little girl for me. I wouldn't care if you had two heads and horns."

She rolled her eyes and crossed her arms over her chest. "I'm an assignment."

"You're so much more than an assignment, Zara. You may have started as an assignment last night when I got the jump drive that contained your information, but that vanished in a heartbeat the moment I set eyes on you."

She shot him another glare. "*See*, you are just interested in me because I'm pretty."

He shook his head. "I'm interested in you because you're bright, funny, and smart. I can also tell that you're submissive and lonely and need a caregiver. I want to be that man, Zara."

"I'm not going to sleep with you," she insisted, even though every molecule in her body knew that wasn't true. She'd never felt this level of attraction for another human being. She'd been fighting it since she'd first turned around in the laundry room and spotted him. Her panties were wet. Good thing she was wearing baggy jeans and a loose shirt because the traitorous breasts that most of the planet coveted and wished they could see more of were currently heavy, her nipples rubbing against the lace of her bra.

And yes, her bra was lacy. So were her panties. Several

years ago, when she'd started hiding from the world in earnest, she'd given up pretty clothes and dresses. She'd exchanged them for ill-fitting shirts and baggy pants.

She had not, however, given up her bra and panty sets. No one ever saw them. Underneath her clothes, she always wore pretty lingerie that allowed her to feel feminine and sexy without drawing attention to herself.

"Nope. You're not going to sleep with me," Kestrel said. "There's a bed for you in the playroom. You'll sleep there where I will know you're safe."

She frowned.

He chuckled. "Go ahead, Little one. Ask me anything. What's your next concern?"

"You don't *want* to sleep with me?" she blurted. It was one thing for her to put her foot down. But he didn't have to agree so quickly without hesitation as if the thought of having her in his bed made him ill.

He chuckled again, his body shaking hers. He cupped her face and held her gaze. "Make no mistake, Zara. I already know I want to be in your life in every way, as your friend, your confidant, your Daddy, your Dom, your lover, and, eventually, your husband. But we'll take this slow. When you come to my bed, you will know definitively that you're there because I'm head over heels in love with you, not because of your looks but because of your heart." He set his other palm on her chest between her breasts.

She stopped breathing. He was so intense and so serious. She wanted to argue with him. None of that was reasonable. They'd just met this morning. He couldn't talk about loving her or marrying her. Could he?

Her skin tingled. Everywhere. There was a force between them. It was real and had a life of its own.

He didn't look away. He held her gaze, rarely blinking.

Her mouth was dry, but she couldn't get the message to her tongue to tell it to lick her lips.

"I'll wait for you, Little one," he continued gently. "For a lifetime, if that's what it takes to convince you I'm not with you for your looks."

She believed him. Or she wanted to. What she knew for sure was she trusted him. He said he would keep her safe, and she needed that. A profound lethargy washed over her as if her body knew instinctively that she could let her guard down with this man. "I'm so tired," she murmured.

He slid his hand around to cup the back of her head. "I bet you are." He kissed her forehead. "Let's get you upstairs so you can take a nap."

He rose, still cradling her in his arms.

She wrapped her arms around his neck, closed her eyes, and let herself feel safe. She inhaled his scent deep into her lungs, loving how he smelled. Memorizing the scent. "You can't carry me upstairs."

"I could. But I won't. I know that would embarrass you. I'll never do anything to embarrass you." He slid her down to her feet but kept his hands on her waist as if making sure she was steady before releasing her.

She glanced at the table. "I should clean this up. We made a mess."

He kissed her forehead again. It felt so good when he did that. "I'll get someone else to do it, Little one."

"I'm not doing laundry anymore. I can do it."

"Celeste has already snapped you up to work with her—but not this morning. You're not on any clock now." He leaned back, smiling.

She sighed and muttered, "I could be."

When he gave her a stern look, she relented slightly. "Fine."

He grabbed her ballcap and settled it back on her head. "Back into hiding, Little Swan."

She scrunched up her face. "Swan?"

"I think it's the perfect nickname for you. You're intelligent, elegant, pure, gentle, and graceful. Those are the qualities of a swan."

She grinned. "You didn't say beautiful."

He shrugged. "That goes without saying." He slid his hands up her back and held her. "I wouldn't care what you looked like, though, Little Swan of mine. When you believe that, then you'll be mine."

He melted her. How did he do that? He tore down her defenses and left her speechless.

"Let's go move your things, and then you can take a nap, yeah?"

"Okay."

Chapter Six

"Come on in, Little Swan," Kestrel encouraged after he used his thumbprint to unlock the entrance to the entire fifth floor. "I'll show you around." He was carrying both of her suitcases. The only things he'd let her carry were her satchel and purse.

When Zara stepped inside, the first thing she noticed was the tall, attractive, dark-skinned man sitting on the largest sectional she'd ever seen. The second thing she noticed made her breath hitch.

A woman was standing in the corner of the room, facing the wall. Zara immediately recognized her from earlier. Wow, had she changed!

Celeste had her hands clasped behind her back. She looked like a child in timeout. Especially since she wore pink leggings, a matching pink cotton dress, and pink tennis shoes. Her hair was in low pigtails at the back of her head.

The man rose from the couch, smiling and extending a hand. "I bet you're Zara. I'm Hawking."

She shook his hand but jerked her gaze downward when she realized she was staring at him. That wasn't like her. She had held his gaze long enough to know he hadn't gawked at her like he'd wanted to make snide comments about her tits or her hair.

Not all men are assholes, Zara. This is one of Kestrel's teammates.

"Sorry, I'm new to all of this," Zara said, waving a hand at Celeste.

"I understand. If you have questions, ask," Hawking said softly. "This is a safe place to be."

Kestrel set her suitcases down and put a hand on her shoulder. "I'm sorry, Hawking. We didn't mean to interrupt."

"Celeste yelled at Magnus today. He'll be up soon to hear her apology. She wasn't ready to say her sorries in the basement. Since her rudeness happened in the common area, so does part of her punishment," Hawking explained.

Zara turned her gaze toward Kestrel.

He smiled. "We don't hide our age play from each other when we're on the fifth floor or in the basement. Naughty Little girls sometimes need a timeout."

Hawking grunted. "This naughty Little girl is going to have trouble sitting down later today."

Zara gasped. Had he spanked her?

"You can turn around now, Little one," Hawking said. "Come assure Zara that you're okay."

Celeste slowly turned around, keeping her head down. Was she embarrassed? She barely resembled the confident scientist Zara had seen on television or in the conference room that morning. That woman had been professionally dressed. This woman was deep in an age-play zone.

Considering Zara hadn't known until a few hours ago that age play was a real thing people actually practiced outside of a book, she was struggling to contain her shock. She finally managed to give a little wave. "Hi."

Celeste bit her lower lip and waved back. "Hey." She turned toward Hawking. "May I go back to work now, Daddy?"

"What do you think, Cuddle Bug?"

She sighed, letting her shoulders drop. "I don't need a nap."

"Do you need *another* spanking?"

"No, Sir." She shook her head.

"Then let's get you tucked in. One hour. Then you can go back to work." He reached out a hand toward her.

Celeste let him take her hand and followed him down the hallway. He opened a door, and they disappeared into what Zara assumed was one of the apartments.

She looked toward Kestrel. "I have so many questions, but why is there a black cat on their door?"

He grinned and nodded in that direction. "Come." He pointed at another door as she followed him. "Sadie and Rocco have a penguin. Celeste likes cats, so she and Hawking have a black cat. We'll have to pick an animal for our door. Do you have a favorite animal? Maybe the swan?"

She shook her head. "I've never thought about swans before. But..." She pursed her lips, hesitating to tell him about Coco.

He lifted a brow. "Do you have a stuffed animal, Little Swan?"

She slowly reached her hand into her satchel, felt along the edge of her computer, and gently removed her most prized possession.

Kestrel reached out to pat him on the head. "Who do we have here?"

"This is Coco, my monkey," she admitted. Never in her wildest dreams had she ever imagined introducing someone to Coco, and certainly not a prospective boyfriend.

Kestrel tickled Coco under the chin before he opened the door they stood next to.

Zara followed him into the apartment, surprised to discover its spaciousness. The living room and kitchen were one great room. There was a short hallway with a few doors off it.

"What do you think?" he asked as he set her suitcases down and flipped on the overhead lights to brighten the room beyond the sunlight through tall windows. "I'll admit I've been busy since arriving here. I haven't done much to make this place a home. You can help me."

She ignored him. Mainly because it still seemed unimaginable to her that she might really stay with him. She'd love to sleep soundly, so she was willing to take him up on his offer of protection, but beyond that? She kept waffling. It was too soon, wasn't it?

"I don't cook much. None of us do. The resort's chefs are amazing. We all eat dinner together each night, usually in the basement. We order most of our other meals from the kitchen or grab something on the run."

Zara turned toward him. "Did Hawking really spank Celeste?"

"I'm sure he did. She works too hard, a lot like someone else I know. She would stay in her lab downstairs twenty hours a day if he didn't put his foot down."

"But she's..."

"Little, Zara. She's Little. She likes having a Daddy guide her and help her make good choices. I can assure you she feels much better after having her bottom spanked. She probably intentionally yelled at Magnus to earn a spanking."

Zara gasped. "Why would she do that?"

He rounded to sit on the sofa and pulled her between his legs, his hands on her hips. He was tall but still had to tip his head back to look at her. "It's cathartic. Lots of people who enjoy age play misbehave when they need the release they get from a spanking."

She swallowed hard. Her mouth was dry again. She couldn't stand still either. Suddenly, all she could think about was Kestrel guiding her to one side of his lap, laying her across his knees, and spanking her. A rush of arousal consumed her and made her already wet panties even wetter.

She jerked her gaze to the side, afraid he could read her face. "Do you want to do that to me?" she whispered.

"Not today, Little Swan, but I'm sure you'll need a good spanking soon." He slid his hands around a few inches and patted her bottom. "You can let me know when your curiosity gets the better of you and ask me to spank you."

She gasped. "Ask you?"

"Yep."

She squirmed. Had he lost his mind?

He set her back a few inches, stood, and took her hand. "Let me show you the rest of the apartment."

All the doors were ajar, and he pushed the first one open. "Master bedroom. Again, I haven't decorated much. It's pretty boring."

She looked around. It was boring. Grays and blacks. No color.

The next door led to a large bathroom. "The bathroom is connected to the bedroom. There's only one in each apartment."

Across the hallway, he opened the last door. "Playroom." He released her and guided her inside with a hand on the small of her back.

The room was furnished but not much else. "Kingsley provided all the playrooms with the basics: desks, daybeds, dressers, bookshelves... But it will be up to you to fix it up the way you want it."

She spun around as she realized what he'd said. "Kingsley bought furniture for adult playrooms?"

"Yes." Kestrel chuckled. "He seems to be intuitive and a bit of a matchmaker." His eyes widened. "Hey, since he's your father's friend, I assume you've met him...?"

She shook her head. "No. I've never met him. I don't even know where he lives. He and my father go way back. He's never come to my family's home. My father has just spoken of him over the years and called him to help protect me."

Kestrel snapped his fingers. "Damn. I was hoping you'd met him."

"You mean you've never met him either?" She set her satchel, purse, and Coco on the desk.

"Nope. None of us have. He's elusive."

"How do you know him then? How did you get hired to work for him?"

"All of us owed him a marker. He got each of us out of a bind at some point in our lives. Sent a team to help us and left a gold coin as a marker, which he recently collected on by calling all of us together here at Danger Bluff."

"Wow. What kind of bind were you in?"

Kestrel hesitated. "It's complicated but I helped a friend protect the woman he loved from traffickers. If it hadn't been for Baldwin Kingsley, I wouldn't have survived."

"Is that why you want to save me? Because you hate traffickers?"

"Yes, and no. Traffickers are the scum of the earth. I would do my best to help anyone threatened by them. You, however, are even more important."

"Because you think I'm your Little?"

"Because I *know* you're my Little girl."

He headed for the daybed. It had a white comforter on it, and he pulled it back. "How about a nap? Later, when you're more rested, I'll take you to the basement to introduce you to everyone else. We'll have dinner together as a family."

She stared at the inviting bed. She considered arguing with him or insisting he tell her more about himself or how he came to be here, but she was so tired that it was difficult to turn down the offer of sleep.

"Let me grab your suitcases. I bet you'd like to change first." He rushed past her and returned seconds later with her baggage. "I'll just open them on the floor for now. We'll unpack your things later."

"I can just live out of them for now," she suggested. It was what she'd been doing so far, anyway. She hadn't unpacked anything in the week since she'd arrived.

He frowned. "This isn't temporary, Little Swan," he said gently.

She bit into her lip again, so badly wanting to believe him. His offer was inviting. Not just protection. He was offering her so much more. His sincerity was evident on his face.

Kestrel unzipped both large suitcases on one side of the room. "Do you have comfortable shorts and T-shirts you could wear for a nap instead of jeans and that long-sleeved shirt?"

She shuffled closer before squatting down and rummaging around until she could grab a matching camisole and sleep shorts set. They were lavender. Thinking again, she dropped them and started looking for something else.

Kestrel was most likely going to see her in whatever she chose. The lavender sleepwear was too revealing.

Kestrel set a hand on her arm and picked up her first option. "This is fine. It looks comfortable." He rose, holding it. "Would you like to go change in the bathroom, Little Swan?"

She couldn't catch her breath. Her heart was suddenly racing as if she'd been jogging. "Uh..."

He lifted a brow. "This offer is for a limited time, Zara. Soon, I will start taking care of you myself. That will include changing you and dressing you in the mornings. But I don't think you're ready for that today. How about if you put these PJs on before I change my mind?"

She snagged them from his hand and rushed to the bathroom. As soon as she was inside and the door shut behind her, she looked in the mirror.

She hardly recognized the woman staring back at her. She jerked off her ballcap and set it on the vanity. It had been a long time since she'd truly looked at herself. Mostly, she'd avoided mirrors lately. They reminded her that she couldn't hide from anyone. Not really.

Today, for the first time in forever, she felt more relaxed in her skin. She stared at her reflection and ran her fingers through her messy hair. It needed to be brushed.

Glancing at the door, she decided she should hurry before Kestrel changed his mind and entered the bathroom. She tugged her ugly shirt over her head while she kicked off her tennis shoes. Next came her jeans. She considered leaving her bra on, but it would be visible through the camisole anyway. Plus, it would be uncomfortable while she napped.

So, she unfastened it, too, and tossed it in the pile of discarded clothes on the floor.

As soon as she had the PJs on, she opened two drawers before locating a brush. It felt so good to brush out her hair.

When she was finished, she looked around and spotted a hamper. Should she put her clothes in there with his? That felt too intimate. Instead, she folded them neatly and carried them back to the bedroom.

Kestrel was sitting on the edge of the daybed. He lifted his gaze and froze.

Don't let it get to you. Don't panic. "Yeah, yeah, I know. I'm pretty." She felt pretty, too. She never let herself feel that way. Not lately. But the way he was looking at her made her knees weak and her pussy wet. He wasn't leering at her like some rabid animal. His gaze was appreciative. He even licked his lips. That pleased her.

"Why didn't you put your clothes in the hamper, Little Swan?" he asked, his voice gravelly.

She glanced over her shoulder toward the bathroom. She was hugging the clothes against her chest, keeping him from seeing her hard nipples. "I wasn't sure..."

"Come here, Little Swan." He reached out a hand.

She went to him. Drawn. She couldn't stop herself. She wanted what he was offering. All of it. Even if it wasn't real, she would pretend, for now, because it felt so good to think someone might care about her, for her, and take care of her in a way she'd only read about in books.

Kestrel took the pile of clothes from her and set it on the floor next to the bed. Without a word, he patted the mattress. "Climb in, Zara."

She quickly climbed under the covers, grateful when he pulled them up to her chin.

He leaned over and kissed her forehead. "Rest, Little Swan. Let yourself relax and get some sleep."

"Thank you." She glanced toward the desk. "Can you get Coco for me?" Kestrel was the only person she'd ever met with whom she felt she didn't have to hide her stuffie.

He grabbed the stuffed monkey, tucked him in with her, and kissed her forehead again. "You're safe now, Zara."

As she watched him reclaim the pile of clothes before leaving the room and pulling the door almost closed, she felt safe. She also felt like one of the heroines in a romance novel. Little. So very Little. It calmed her.

It usually took forever to fall asleep, but she drifted off as soon as she closed her eyes.

Chapter Seven

Pulling his phone out of his pocket, he checked the device for his schedule. *Damn!* He had to take a group on a sightseeing flight in twenty minutes. Kestrel dropped her clothes on the hidden washer off the main living space and set her cell phone on the coffee table. He knew she hadn't seen him palm the device as he'd handed her Coco. After setting a pillow on top of the phone in case she'd set an alarm in the bathroom, Kestrel jotted Zara a note quickly and added that on top of the pile. Letting himself out of the apartment, Kestrel jogged to the elevator.

Once outside, he called Magnus as he hurried toward the helipad.

"I wondered if you'd remember you have some groups?" the computer expert remarked drily.

"Groups. Crap! I just saw this one," Kestrel lamented.

"It's tough to work, isn't it?"

"I know. You live online, keeping track of everyone and everything. We all appreciate it. Could I ask a favor?" Kestrel requested.

"Maybe."

"Zara just went down for a nap. I left her a note but asked her to wait for me in the upstairs social area. Is there a backup sensor on the fifth floor in the living space that you could activate?"

"I can. It's turned off for privacy but I'll flip it on for a few hours."

"Thanks. When she walks in and triggers it, would you help her get down the elevator to the basement? She's interested in working with Celeste."

"Celeste's not down here either," Magnus informed him.

"Hawking won't be able to make her nap for long. Celeste is much too excited about the project she's working on." Kestrel was running out of time to make arrangements. He was almost at the place where he would meet his tour group.

"You're right. So, you want me to be the voice of all power and lure her to the basement? Think she's seen any horror movies?" Magnus asked.

"Do your best, Magnus. Channel your inner Daddy. Just remember, she's mine."

"Gotcha. I'll watch for her," Magnus promised. "Pay attention to the weather. There's a storm brewing. You should be okay today, but the rest of the week is going to be dodgy."

"Thanks, Magnus."

Kestrel slowed to a walk as he approached a group that appeared to be a family. "Hi! I'm Kestrel. Are you here for the helicopter tour?"

"Hi, Kestrel. We're excited!" a woman said, returning his greeting. "It's a cracker."

When Kestrel looked at her in confusion, she laughed.

"Sorry. You're from the United States, right? A cracker is a gorgeous sunny day for us here in New Zealand."

"A cracker, huh? I like that. So, we should get cracking, huh?"

"We can't wait."

Twenty minutes later, Kestrel skillfully set the helicopter back down on the landing pad as if he were landing on a cotton ball as the family clapped. After helping the last guest out of the aircraft, he got a message through his earpiece.

"She's still sleeping."

He lifted his hand and gave the security camera over the helipad area a thumbs up. Thank goodness for Magnus.

Kestrel finally had a break after his third group. After smiling for pictures with the chattering group, he jogged back to the main house while calling Magnus again. "Any update, Magnus?"

Zara's voice came through the speakerphone. "I'm down here, Kestrel, with Celeste."

He smiled at the strength in her voice. She sounded so much better. He bet her last good night's sleep had been back at her parents' house. Slowing as he reached the resort's front entrance, Kestrel headed inside toward the elevator.

"Kestrel!" Sadie waved at him from the front desk. "I've got a change in your schedule. It's updated for you, too, but I didn't want you to miss it," she explained.

"I have another flight now?" he asked, pulling out his phone to double-check.

"You've got an hour and a half. Someone asked to move their flight back because their arrival got bumped back by a problem at the airport. You'll finish up a bit later but still make it for dinner," she summed up for him.

"Perfect. Thanks, Sadie."

"I like her, Kestrel."

"I do, too. Coming for lunch?" he asked. Everyone gathered for dinner. Lunch was a hit-or-miss thing, depending on everyone's schedule.

"I wouldn't miss it. Magnus just called for fish and chips for a crowd," Sadie said with a laugh.

Kestrel smirked as he walked to the elevator. Their health-conscious tech guy had called for deep-fried food? He must have let Zara choose. He might seem cold and remote, but Magnus had a soft spot for Littles.

When he reached the bottom floor, Kestrel found Magnus at his desk. His "Thanks, Magnus!" received a nod as the other man worked diligently on something.

He followed the sound of feminine voices to the lab area they'd set up for Celeste. The scientist's equipment had overwhelmed the small area she'd started working in. The guys had brought in experts to create a professional-grade lab complete with protective devices like exhaust fans and shielded workspaces.

Having them complete the work and keep the guests unaware of the basement had been a challenge. Magnus had found a trusted team that worked on security-sensitive projects. They'd brought in all the equipment and supplies through the back doors in the wee hours of the morning.

"Hi, ladies," Kestrel said as he joined the two women discussing something he was sure was important. Celeste had recently made a major discovery that would bring the scientific community miles closer to developing a cure for cancer. Anything she was involved in had to be earth-shattering.

Both women looked at him. Zara took a step his way and froze. Kestrel solved the problem for her and crossed the distance between them to wrap his arm around her waist. "Hi, Zara."

"Hi...Kestrel."

He loved that she had hesitated. She must have already been thinking of him as "Daddy" but had stopped herself. She'd be ready on her own time.

He nodded toward Celeste next. "Hi, Celeste." He stopped and looked at their faces. "You both look rested. Do you feel better?"

"Don't tell Hawking, but I got back down here to the lab and figured out the problem that had me up all night," Celeste admitted.

"He doesn't have to tell me," a deep voice sounded from the doorway.

"Daddy!"

Celeste flew across the lab into Hawking's arms. He hugged her close and pressed a kiss to her temple. "I'm glad you feel better, and your mind is sharp. That's the bit of proof I needed to implement a daily nap for you, Cuddle Bug."

"Daddy," Celeste started to complain but snapped her mouth closed when Hawking patted her bottom lightly. "Okay. I do feel better."

"Dr. Blanke is working on incredible things here," Zara commented to help deflect the attention from the scientist.

"Zara, no more Dr. Blanke. If you're going to work with me, I need you to call me Celeste," the scientist corrected her firmly.

"Got it. Celeste," Zara agreed quickly.

"It's lunchtime. I just brought down enough fish and chips for an army," Hawking said. "Come help me, Celeste."

Kestrel nodded his thanks as Hawking arranged for him to have a bit of private time with Zara. "Did you and Coco sleep well?"

"I did. The whole morning is gone. I should've woken up earlier," Zara apologized with pink cheeks. He suppressed a laugh when she rallied to add, "If you hadn't taken my phone, I would've woken up sooner."

"You're supposed to sleep, Little Swan."

"But not like forever!"

"As long as you need. Your phone will go in the box on the coffee table when we enter our apartment."

"What if I want to call my parents?" she asked.

"Are you supposed to call your parents?"

She sighed deeply and shook her head. "Only in an emergency."

"Then sleep is more important because you'll be safe with me. If you would like, we could ask Magnus if there is a way to contact your parents without exposing your location."

"That would be amazing. Can we go ask now?" She tugged at his arm, trying to pull him to the door.

"If he's eating, let's ask later. He deserves a break, too," Kestrel reminded her.

"Oh. Of course. A few minutes won't matter. I'm sure they know I'm here, but I know my mother is worrying."

"We'll see what we can do, but first, a kiss. Second, lunch."

"Thank you, Daddy," Zara whispered before rising onto her tiptoes to press her mouth against his.

His heart lurched in his chest at the feel of her lips. He didn't deepen the kiss but allowed her to be in charge. To his delight, Zara whisked her tongue over the inner line of his sensitive bottom lip. Opening his mouth to invite her in, Kestrel pulled her closer. Her tongue darted into his mouth and danced with his.

Kestrel's body responded to the kiss and her closeness. He trapped a groan in his throat when she wiggled against his pelvis. He didn't want to interrupt or scare her away. She froze in place a second later, and he knew she felt his shaft thickening.

"Oh! I'm sorry," she said, backing away.

He controlled her motion and met her skittish gaze, holding it. "Never be ashamed of how our bodies welcome each other."

"I've never..."

"I know. Making love to the woman I know is my Little will be a first for me as well. I might be a bit nervous, too."

"Really?"

"Yes. I want to be everything for you."

She thought for a minute and then smiled. "That sounds nice."

"Our lovemaking will be everything but something as simple as *nice*. My body responds to you. I would bet yours does as well. Are you wet, Little Swan?"

"Yes," she whispered.

"See? Much more than nice."

To his surprise, she leaned forward to kiss him hard. The exchange was filled with heat and desire. They were both breathing hard when she lifted her lips. "You're right. It will be so much more."

Chapter Eight

Zara had to struggle to pull her attention away from thoughts of Kestrel. *Daddy,* she corrected herself mentally. Would she be able to call him Daddy around the others?

"I can hear you thinking all the way over here," Celeste told her.

"Sorry. I thought I had a lot going on before I met Kestrel and all of you. Now..."

"I'm sorry. We were all there when the flash drive arrived from Mr. Kingsley," Celeste shared.

"So, you all know that people are after me to sell for someone's use. I don't even want to think that the world is so cruel that people like that exist," Zara said with tears gathering in her eyes.

"No crying on the test samples," Celeste warned. "They can leak through the safety goggles. Don't ask me how I know."

Zara backed away from the work table, making sure she couldn't mess anything up. "I'm so sorry. You need someone professional in here."

"Are you kidding? If you try to walk out that door, I'm going to tackle you. Then I'll get in trouble and get spanked. Daddy will make me apologize, and we'll waste so much time."

Bombarded by the rapid-fire speech, Zara stared at Celeste in amazement. "You know exactly what would happen?"

"At least one probability. So, no bailing, okay? I need your help, and I'm glad to have a new friend. Come over here and test the pH of these samples. Yes, use those," Celeste confirmed as Zara pointed to the testing strips.

After stripping off her gloves, Zara wiped her eyes and resettled her goggles on her face. She tugged on new gloves and joined Celeste. "I'm glad to have a friend, too."

The two worked together extremely well. Time passed quickly. Zara glanced at the door when she heard something slam into the concrete. Heart racing, she looked at Celeste to judge her reaction.

"That's just Magnus working out. He's a beast."

"I saw the workout corner. They're all in good shape," Zara murmured.

"Prime eye candy."

The two women burst into laughter, automatically moving to a safer area away from their work. They leaned against the door, giggling.

Secure in the basement, learning from an amazing scientist, and getting to experiment, Zara felt like she was finally living. It was an incredible feeling. When they wrapped up for the day, she realized all she wanted to do was tell Kestrel everything. He was her first thought, not her folks. Her mind felt totally unbalanced. How could he have become the most important person in her life so quickly?

"Don't fight it," Celeste counseled without provocation. "I can see the wheels going a million kilometers an hour in your mind. It's okay just to enjoy having Kestrel in your life. I can't imagine how things would be for me without Hawking."

Taking a deep breath, Zara exhaled and pushed away all her hovering fears. Maybe, for once, she could take someone at their word.

"Little girl!" Kestrel wrapped his arms around Zara, hugging her as he lifted her from her feet.

"Daddy!" she protested and then clapped her hand over her mouth as she looked around.

"No one cares, Little Swan. Well, the guys that haven't found their Little girls are jealous, but they aren't judging you for being Little," Kestrel assured her.

Zara nodded and looked back again at everyone. Sadie sat on her Daddy's lap, talking between kisses. Magnus was at his computer now that his workout was finished. Celeste rested against Hawking, who leaned against the wall. He rubbed her back as his Little relaxed against him. Phoenix and Caesar were getting the table ready for everyone's dinner. It looked like a big family.

She looked back at Kestrel. He had lines around his eyes that he didn't usually have. "You look tired."

"I am tired. I had a bunch of flights together without the usual break because of some scheduling issues. I was just glad to get to have dinner with you," he explained.

"What do you do on a flight?" she asked.

"You'll have to come with me when we have a space."

"Is that allowed?" Then, shaking her head, she added, "It's probably not safe."

"Dinner time," Phoenix announced from behind.

He'd obviously heard part of their discussion because he asked, "Why couldn't you take all the Littles up? Sadie could create a special time for you."

"Oh, I don't want to make you have to work more," Zara said quickly.

"That's not a problem. I love flying. The difficulty will be keeping you unnoticed and safe," Kestrel shared. "Let's have dinner, and the team will try to figure out how to make that happen."

She allowed Kestrel to guide her to the table and sat next to him. As everyone settled in their spots, Kestrel leaned over to say, "Just so you know, we all talk about something as we help ourselves to the main course."

"What?" she asked, totally confused.

"You'll see."

"Magnus, you start," Rocco suggested.

"Damn speaking spoon," Magnus muttered as he lifted the ladle from the large container of potato soup. "I searched for any threats or rumbles on the web today. There was nothing specific but some chatter got my attention. I'll continue to follow up. The weather is also ramping up, so we need to make sure the resort is ready for a big storm, possibly at the end of the week."

He handed the spoon to Phoenix. The large man said, "The resort didn't have a weather emergency plan. My crews will start weather-proofing the resort slowly so that everything stays open until the last moment. Guests will want to enjoy all the amenities."

Sadie stood to make it easier to dip soup from the container. When she hesitated, Rocco moved to help her.

Grinning, Sadie picked up her smaller metal spoon to take her turn.

"Thanks, Daddy. Everything is going well on the guests' side of the resort. We're about two-thirds full, which is spectacular. Most are here with reservations, but we always have a few families that show up, hoping we have space. Today, we had three men come in separately. That was a bit strange, but from what I see, they're vacationing."

Zara felt Kestrel tense next to her. "What were they doing?" he asked.

"One went to the pool. Another walked the grounds. There was one in your helicopter today," Sadie shared. "I'll let you know if I see anything concerning. Oh, and Mark tracked me down to see if I'd seen Zara. He was concerned about her. I told him she was enjoying her new job."

"He was very nice to me while I worked in the laundry room," Zara commented. Mark had been interesting. He'd never looked at her as anything other than average.

"He must miss you working so hard," Kestrel added.

When Sadie held the spoon out to Rocco, he accepted it with a smile and a "Thank you, Cookie. Guess it's my turn." Taking a moment, Rocco ladled himself some soup before adding, "Nothing exciting is happening on the bluff side. I think I had one of those single men today in a rock-climbing class. When he saw we weren't going very high on the bluff, he wanted to know when the advanced class was. He wants to get a view of the area from above. Magnus, can you do a bit of digging into these guys?"

"Got them tagged as they arrived," Magnus confirmed.

"Do you think they're after me somehow?" Zara blurted. "Sorry. I don't have the spoon, but I can't wait to ask."

"The spoon is our way of keeping up with each other, Zara. It's just a fun way to report what's going on, and everyone listens. You can always ask questions," Rocco assured her as Kestrel wrapped an arm around her.

"Zara, we're alert for any type of threat. Anything that seems out of the norm," Kestrel shared. "The team is working together to make sure you're safe."

"Here, Kestrel," Rocco handed over the ladle.

"Lots of families on the sightseeing trips. Everyone takes photos, but I noticed that the single guy on one trip was taking specific photos of the roads into the estate and the sea access. It was like he was scouting the area. Here, Little Swan. Tell us about your day."

"I'm scared now," she started, looking into the faces of these people she didn't know but who seemed dedicated to saving her. "The rest of my day was great. I got moved into a new room up on the fifth floor. I haven't slept well, so someone made me nap." The response from the Daddies made her smile.

"Good job."

"Of course!"

"You needed it."

"Sleep is good for you."

"Great!"

"Did it help?" Kestrel asked softly.

Zara cleared her throat and admitted. "Yes. I had enough brain power to work with Celeste in the lab. I enjoyed it so much."

"And you did an amazing job," Celeste said with a smile.

The sharing continued through the remainder of the people, and soon, everyone dived into the delicious meal. It felt almost like home. Zara was amazed that this group had become a family with traditions and rituals. She'd learned so much about the entire team.

Kestrel wrapped his left hand around her thigh and

squeezed just a bit. She smiled up at him, trying not to worry about what the future would bring. Automatically, she opened her mouth as he lifted his spoon to offer her a bite. Then, feeling funny as he fed her, she looked around the table. No one watched. They were all chatting and having a good time. Sadie had even moved from her chair to sit on Rocco's lap.

"It's really okay here, isn't it?" she whispered into Kestrel's ear.

"Yes, Little Swan. Your heart is safe here."

As soon as dinner was over, the men took over and shooed the Littles from the table. Unable to help, the women gathered in the living space. Zara felt awkward. Her family had employed a staff over the years to handle everything in the house. Here, she felt that she should do something.

"Don't worry about it, Zara," Celeste said when she caught her new friend looking over her shoulder repeatedly to where the men joked around in the dining room as they cleaned and organized the dishes back on the cart to go upstairs.

"They like hanging together as much as we do," Sadie mentioned with a laugh as Rocco popped Hawking on the butt with a kitchen towel. "Daddy's going to be in trouble."

Kestrel threw himself between the two men as they tried to get at each other. Zara couldn't help but laugh at their antics. "They've been a group for a long time," she stated.

"Oh, not too long. They're all ex-military, so they like working with others they know have their backs," Sadie pointed out. "They'd all do anything for each other or us."

Zara covered her mouth as she yawned. "Sorry. I shouldn't be tired."

"That's it for you tonight," Kestrel said, holding his hand out for hers. "We're going to have an early night."

"But..." Zara began before a huge yawn interrupted her statement. "Okay," she conceded. She felt dead on her feet. "Night, everyone."

Waves and wishes for a good night's sleep answered her as Kestrel guided her to the elevator.

Chapter Nine

Leaning against her Daddy's hard body on the way up to their floor, she stared at the numbers going past. "Daddy, why doesn't the elevator stop for other people? We're always the only ones in here."

"There's a magic fairy controlling the doors."

"I'm going to tell Magnus you called him a magic fairy," Zara teased, quickly figuring out who he was talking about.

"Go ahead. I'm pretty sure he has a magic wand."

"Daddy, he has his computer."

"Computer...wand...same difference," Kestrel suggested with a shrug as he steered her out of the elevator.

Feeling nervous and excited to be alone with him, Zara tried to keep her mind busy as they entered his apartment. "What do you do in the evenings?"

"I paint rocks."

"Rocks?" she repeated.

"Yes. Here, I have one for you." Kestrel left her side to walk to an end table with a single drawer. Opening it, he pulled out a small object which he hid in his hand.

"What is it?" Zara asked, holding her hand out as he returned.

Kestrel set a smooth rock about two inches across on her palm. It was vaguely shaped like a heart, and he had accentuated this by painting the entire surface pink and adding a large red heart placed to match the contours. In the middle was written *Daddy's Girl.*

"I thought I would add our initials over here," he said, pointing to a sliver of extra space on the side. "I'll do that tomorrow."

"Where are you going to put the rock when it's done?" she asked.

This concept was not alien to Zara. Growing up in both Mexico and the States, she'd seen painted rocks placed in visible spots for people to see. Some were sneakier than others, but all had made her smile. She didn't really know why, but the unexpected find always made her happy.

"I'm going to give it to you. I thought you might like it in your playroom. I've found my Little girl. It's hers to keep," Kestrel said softly.

"Thank you!" Holding it to her heart, Zara headed toward the room where she'd napped. She stopped when Kestrel gently caught her arm.

"Bath first. Then I'll tuck you into bed."

She moaned at the thought of lounging in a sudsy tub. "That sounds like heaven."

"Come on. I'll start the water."

Following him into the master bathroom, she watched him turn on the faucet in the tub. "Um, I can do it."

"Little Swan. You're so tired. Can you let your Daddy help?" Kestrel asked, cupping her face.

"But..."

"I'm going to give you a bath to help you sleep. You can

trust me not to do anything you're not ready for," Kestrel promised.

"I've never..."

"I know. I'll take care of you, I promise."

"Okay," she whispered.

Kestrel pulled the baggy shirt over her head, revealing a hot pink bra. It was beautiful with lace and satin. She watched him smile. "I like lingerie. I can't wear anything fancy that anyone else can see, so I always have pretty underthings."

"Now, I can't wait to see if you have matching panties," he teased.

She nodded as he knelt at her feet to strip off her shoes and socks. Then, Kestrel unfastened her pants and drew them over her curved hips. He helped her step out of the material before standing. Stroking a finger over the lacy waistband, he said, "You may just be the best present I've ever unwrapped."

When she felt her skin heat from his compliment, Zara knew she was blushing. Her mind seized on his words. He didn't compliment her beauty or fixate on her body. He was pleased that she was girly underneath everything.

"This needs to go before the bath." With deft motions, Kestrel freed her from her bra and slid the panties down her legs.

He groaned and shifted himself inside his slacks, drawing her attention to the tented material. "Let's get you in the tub. Choose bubbles. I ordered these when I moved in, just in case. Would you like bubble gum or lavender?"

"Lavender, please."

He poured a small amount into the tub, which instantly bubbled into a relaxing fragrance that filled the room. "Into the tub. By the time you're settled, there will be a perfect amount of foam."

"Bubbles, Daddy," she corrected as she stepped into the tub with his assistance and sat down with a delighted sigh. "This is heaven."

Kestrel opened a cabinet and pulled out two washcloths. "Lie back against the tub. This will keep the light from shining in your eyes." He gently placed one of the cloths over her eyes.

She could hear him settling next to the tub. To her surprise, she discovered that not seeing helped free her. He dipped the second washcloth into the water and lifted one leg to wash her toes and foot. Zara bit her bottom lip to hold back the moan of enjoyment at being so pampered.

"Daddy needs to hear your sounds," he corrected gently. "No biting."

Instantly, she followed his request and realized she wanted to please him. Following his directions allowed her to be Little. He was in charge. She smiled.

"I like the look on your face. You must be having a sweet thought," he commented as he washed her calf.

The smooth soap coated the skin of her outer thigh as he continued his path. She gasped slightly as he washed her inner thigh. Zara wrinkled her nose in disappointment when he skimmed over her private places as he switched to the other leg and repeated the path in reverse.

"No worries, Little Swan. I won't forget any part of you."

Her mind spun at that statement. What did he mean?

When he placed her other foot back into the water, the anticipation of where he would go next pushed away her worries. He lifted her hand from the water and smoothed the silky cleanser into her skin, massaging away the slight ache from holding equipment tightly so she wouldn't make a mistake in the lab. It felt so much better as he moved up her arm. His fingers brushed the outer curve of her breast, making her gasp.

"So sensitive, Little Swan. Are you enjoying my touch?"

She hesitated and then whispered, "Yes."

"It's not enough?" he probed.

She shook her head, dislodging the shield over her eyes slightly. He adjusted it with damp, sweet-smelling hands. *I love this so much.* "Thank you."

"You're welcome, Little girl. Let's see. Where was I?"

She held her breath, imagining him looking over her as he tried to recall where he had last washed her body. His fingers retraced his path—up one leg, down the next, skip to her hand, and up the inside of her arm. She shivered as he once again brushed the side of her breast.

"Oh, yes. This is where I stopped."

He continued cleaning her skin, smoothing over her shoulder and across her collarbones to the other side. Zara held as still as possible so she didn't dislodge the cloth over her eyes. His touch was so difficult to resist.

When he reached her fingers on the other side, Kestrel repeated his massage of her hands as she melted against the porcelain tub. As he lowered her fingers back into the water, she held her breath. What would he wash next?

She felt his hand press the cloth over her eyes to hold it in place. "Lean forward, Little Swan," he softly directed as he helped her move into the position he wanted.

Slow, smooth strokes over her back made her groan with pleasure.

"That feels good, doesn't it?" he asked and pressed a kiss to the top of her head as he continued washing all the way to her bottom.

When he helped her settle back against the tub, she

sighed in disappointment. She didn't want it to end. The touch of the washcloth on her neck totally dispersed her regret. He gripped her throat and held her firmly for a second before sliding the cloth around the back of her neck. That brief feeling of having her breath constricted was a spark to the arousal growing inside.

"Hmmm? Your pulse increased, Little Swan. I can see it pounding right here." His fingers traced over the artery.

"Daddy..."

"I know. Bath time can be exciting. It's okay, Little one. I'm here to take care of you."

He swirled the cloth down the midline of her body. The edges brushed over the inside curve of her breasts, increasing her arousal. Zara squeezed her legs together, trying to control it. Kestrel didn't allow that. He stroked the washcloth up her torso to cup one breast. His finger or thumb swept the wet material across her nipple over and over again until she moaned.

"So responsive," he praised before repeating the process on the other side.

She was not at all ready for him to move on when he drew the cloth down her body again. A whimper of protest escaped, embarrassing her, but the kiss that landed on her forehead reassured her.

"Spread your legs, Zara," he requested. His firm tone didn't allow her to do anything but comply.

Slowly, she drew her knees up and let them fall slightly open. He pressed her knees to the sides of the tub with warm, wet hands. "Just like that, Little Swan."

He swished the washcloth over her small mound before gliding it lightly down her cleft. The second pass was closer to her core as he dipped cloth-covered fingers into her pink folds. He didn't stop there. The material continued farther down her body, gliding between her buttocks to brush over that small hidden entrance. The textured fabric rasped over the nerve-rich target repeatedly as she struggled not to move —not to react.

"It's okay, Zara. Daddy knows."

She shivered in reaction to that reassurance. How could he read her mind? How did he know exactly what she was feeling and needing?

Zara felt a whisp of fabric touch her ankle before Kestrel caressed her with his fingertips, the washcloth disappearing as he touched her directly. The breath caught in her throat as he explored her body. Each touch pushed her closer to something she didn't quite understand—but wanted so badly.

Zings of pleasure assaulted her, buffeting her body as he built on the fire already sizzling inside her. She reached out a hand, needing to tether herself to him. Blindly floundering, she felt his warm skin and wrapped her hand around his thick bicep. Her fingers clamped down as she held on with all her strength.

"*Yessss!*" she screamed into the room. Her voice echoed against the hard surfaces of the bathroom as she twisted in the water.

He softened his touch and gathered her in his arms, lifting her seemingly effortlessly from the tub to stand in front of him. The fabric fell away from her eyes, and she stared into his face as he wrapped her in a thick, thirsty towel. His expression seared itself into her memory. Fierce passion and possession carved themselves in his features as his gaze blazed with heat. She lifted a hand to cup his face, and he turned his mouth to her palm to sear it with a kiss.

"Daddy?"

"You are so precious, Zara."

Carefully, he dried her skin and wrapped her in the

towel. "Bedtime, Little girl. Do you want to sleep with Daddy or in your playroom?"

"Daddy," she said before she could talk herself out of it.

"I'm glad. Let me tuck you in, and then I'll get Coco for you to hold while I take the coldest shower ever recorded."

"Cold?" she repeated, not understanding.

Kestrel drew her forward to press against his body. Even through the thick toweling, she could feel how hard he was everywhere. *He's not that big, is he?*

Her shock must have shown on her face because he nodded and explained, "Zara, you affect Daddy as much as his touch turned you on."

"Umm... Should I help you—somehow? I don't know what to do, but you could coach me."

With a groan, he moved her away from him. "I promise I'll show you everything. We'll learn to please each other together just like we did tonight. But now, it's time for Little girls to be in bed. Come on, Little Swan."

As he promised, he tucked her into bed and zipped into the playroom to retrieve Coco. "Close your eyes, Little girl. I'll join you in a few minutes."

"Yes, Daddy."

Exhausted mentally and physically, Zara rolled onto her tummy and pulled Coco close. She heard him moving around quietly for a while. It was reassuring not being alone. *Daddy.*

Chapter Ten

Waking the next morning to find his arms filled with delicious curves, Kestrel stared at the ceiling for a second to make sure he wasn't still dreaming. Satisfied by the old-fashioned light above him, Kestrel risked glancing to his left. A laugh escaped from his lips as he looked straight into brown, fuzzy eyes. Coco's eyes.

"Daddy?"

"Hi, Zara. I didn't mean to wake you," Kestrel said softly as he lifted Coco higher on the pillows and looked down his body to see his Little girl.

Tucked close, she still rested her cheek against his chest. Slowly, she inched her leg down from its position over his pelvis. Kestrel grinned. *Like I'm not going to notice.*

"You didn't wake me," she stated and then yawned, betraying the truth.

"Try that again, Little Swan. It's not a good idea to start the day with a lie."

"I wasn't really lying," she said, looking up at him with wide, crystal-blue eyes.

As soon as their gazes locked, she nodded and admitted, "Okay. I was dozing, but that's almost asleep."

"I'm sorry, Little girl. I woke up, and Coco was staring at me."

"He does that sometimes. He's always keeping vigil over me. That's why I love him so much."

"I'm glad he takes such good care of you. He was definitely checking me out to make sure I wasn't a bad guy."

"Oh, I'll talk to him." She propped herself up on one elbow to look for Coco and, in the process, nudged Kestrel in a sensitive area.

"Oof!" He grabbed her knee and moved it to a safer spot.

"Oh! I'm sorry!" she said, scrambling back away from him and almost doing more damage.

Kestrel quickly wrapped his arms around her and held her plastered on top of his body. She froze in place as their naked bodies pressed intimately together. "You're going to kill me, Little Swan."

"I'm sorry," she said with tears gathering in her eyes.

Immediately, he felt like he'd mistreated a kitten. "Zara, I should be the one apologizing. I didn't mean to make you feel bad. I'm teasing."

"Really? I didn't hurt you?"

"There are some areas on a man just like a woman that are very sensitive. You may have caused a temporary twinge but you didn't hurt me, Zara."

"Promise?"

"I promise."

"I should get off you before I hurt you again," she suggested and wiggled before freezing. "Could you help me so I don't hurt you?"

She was so earnest, he couldn't resist. Rolling their bodies entwined together, he reversed their positions so he was on top. Kestrel balanced his weight on a knee braced between her thighs and his forearm. "All better."

"I still can't move," she whispered after tentatively squirming a bit.

"Maybe I like having you right here," Kestrel suggested. He brushed her silky hair away from her face. "Do you like being with Daddy?"

She nodded and reached up to run her hands over his shoulders. Kestrel loved how she traced the muscles as she learned his body. He lowered his head to capture her mouth, and she slid her hand over her mouth.

"Morning breath," she mumbled.

"Does that mean my breath is stinky?" he asked in amusement.

"Oh! No. I was talking about myself," she assured him, pulling her hand away.

To his delight, she lifted her head to press her lips lightly against his. Kestrel allowed her to be in control until she pulled back.

"Take a breath, Little girl," he ordered.

"A breath?"

"Your lips won't be free for a while," he warned, and then her chest rose against him as she inhaled. "Good girl."

Kestrel kissed her lips softly before deepening the kiss gradually. He loved her taste. Trying not to scare her, he held himself back. When she lifted a hand to weave it through his hair to tug him closer, he threw caution to the wind. To his delight, her tongue met his and traced around it in a cat-and-mouse game that gave him a glorious reason to explore her mouth. They were both breathing heavily when he lifted his head.

"Are you going to make love to me?" she whispered.

Instantly any other plans vanished from his mind as he

lowered his lips to hers once again. An annoying sound began but Kestrel ignored it. Nothing was more important than this. This time her hand tugged his hair, drawing his mouth from hers.

"Your phone is ringing," she told him hesitantly.

"Just strike me with lightning," he requested to the heavens as he rolled over to silence his phone. The sight of Sadie's name made him answer.

"You have a flight in exactly nine minutes," she informed him crisply.

Kestrel could hear the giggle she was hiding with her professional voice. Cursing silently, he knew that he had to maintain his cover as the others did. "I'll be there. You're killing me, Little girl," he growled into the phone before he hung up, turning back to face Zara.

"Hey! Don't sleep through your flight!" a deep voice shouted through the door to his apartment.

They're ganging up on me.

"Sorry, Little Swan. It will be our time soon. I promise," Kestrel said, throwing himself out of bed.

Her gasp made him freeze, afraid something had happened. To his delight, Zara stared squarely at his erection. Her mouth rounded into a perfect O.

"Eyes on mine, Little girl."

"That's never going to fit," she told him with a shocked look on her face.

"It will fit. And I'll make sure you enjoy it even more than your bath," Kestrel said before he forced himself to jog to the dresser for athletic briefs he usually wore to work out in. He was going to need all the layers of stretchy support and disguise he could get.

In two minutes, he was dressed with his hair and teeth brushed and tugging on his shoes. "Go have fun with Celeste today. I'll be back for lunch unless my schedule is messed up again. If so, I'll see you at dinner," he promised.

With one last hard kiss, he forced himself out the door and into the elevator. Hawking caught the doors at the last moment and stepped in with him. "Tough morning?"

"Don't even start. I remember when Celeste first got here," Kestrel reminded him.

"I'm glad Zara's here. There's no doubt she's yours?"

"From the first time I saw her."

"I don't know what Kingsley is doing, but I hope he keeps it up," Hawking remarked.

The doors opened, and the two men stepped out into the hotel lobby. Kestrel took the time to nod his agreement before jogging out of the hotel and toward the location where he picked up his riders. He would confirm the riders on his phone with the list Sadie kept updated. Above all, he'd plot just exactly what he was going to do to Zara when he had her alone.

It was going to be a long day.

Chapter Eleven

"Here, man." Phoenix brought Kestrel a sandwich for lunch when he couldn't get back to the resort to grab something.

"You're a lifesaver. I missed breakfast this morning, and I was stupid enough to add an extra flight during my usual lunch break," Kestrel bemoaned as he opened the sub sandwich wrapper and took a huge bite.

"Slow down. If you choke, I'll have to give you the Heimlich, and I don't know if I like you that much," Phoenix joked.

"You'd save me."

"You sound pretty confident of that," Phoenix commented with a smile that neither denied nor confirmed Kestrel's assertion.

"Your Little is coming. You'll want me around to help keep her safe."

"Damn, right. I want her wrapped in cotton and safe from everything," Phoenix confirmed. "Why do you think I didn't let you starve? I have to get back to my role here. Do chew a bit."

"Thanks, Mom."

Kestrel watched the big man walk away. They'd never talked about what each man had done during their time in the military. He didn't know why he thought of tanks when he saw Phoenix. The man looked like he could carry a couple.

He took several more bites of his sandwich as he saw his next customers heading his way. Stowing the remains carefully in a cooler for later, he greeted the resort guests and prepared to go over the safety precautions. The trickiest part of the flight was getting out when they returned. Everyone was ready to rush out. He reminded them repeatedly throughout the flight to duck as they stepped out of the helicopter and to never raise their hands above their heads. Flying sunglasses were better lost than fingers cut away by the rotors.

There was one repeat customer. Kestrel didn't like how he watched everything. Not the scenery up in the sky, but he seemed to be scoping out the setup of the helicopter pad. His gaze skated over the cooler of water that the employees brought for Kestrel and any guests who might feel queasy after the flight. He looked at the control for the helipad and the locking system designed to keep anyone from deciding to take a joyride in the middle of the night. Kestrel opened a panel he knew would set an alarm off, and immediately it went out.

Hawking spoke through his earpiece. "Problem?"

"Ask Magnus to check the ninety-degree box." That would be enough code for the computer guru to focus on the man standing across from him. He would understand that Kestrel had noticed something suspicious.

Then, he spoke to his riders. "Thank goodness, that only controls the air conditioning inside the booth. We have our own air vents up there."

"Would that be the wind?" a teenager asked, trying to look totally bored.

"You got it. We've got a few gusts up there pushing the clouds out of our way so we'll get the best view. This is your lucky day. Ready to go? Want to be in front with me?" he asked the teenager.

"Yes! I mean, that would be fine," he answered, trying to play off his excitement as his parents and sister hid their grins.

As soon as he got everyone loaded and the engines turned on, he fit his headphones over his ears and motioned everyone to do the same. He asked everyone to check their seat belts and give him a thumbs up that they could hear him. "I'll tell the controllers that we're taking off."

He switched to a different frequency while resting his hand over the display on the dial so the man sitting behind him couldn't see the numbers. Covering his mouth with his other hand as if that made the sound reach the controllers faster, his real purpose was to make sure the man couldn't read his lips.

Kestrel asked, "You there, Magnus?"

"Got him. I'll do some digging. Let me know when you can what spooked you."

"Will do."

Grateful that Magnus had understood to look ninety degrees from his location as they stood talking, Kestrel knew he'd have the guy's third-grade teacher's name when they got back, as well as truly important information about his life. Magnus was thorough. *I'm glad he's on my side.*

Looking at his watch as he jogged to the main building, Kestrel tried to judge if he had enough time to pick up Zara from the basement and take her upstairs for some alone time before dinner. No, he definitely wanted more than a quickie. Kestrel cursed the extra time he'd taken to exceed the requirements to secure the helicopter in place. The guy had rattled him. He planned to ask Magnus to block him from scheduling any more flights.

Heading downstairs, he found everyone already seated around the table. The food hadn't arrived, but everyone was sitting and chatting. Zara sat in his chair. Her hair was piled on her head, with corkscrew curls rioting around her face.

"Kestrel! About time you got here," Caesar called, waving his beer.

"You look rough, buddy," he replied.

"This is my third shirt today. The waters were choppy, and not everyone's stomach was cooperating," the scuba instructor shared.

"Ugh. Thank goodness you have an endless supply. And a wet suit to put on," Kestrel sympathized.

"Let's not even talk about that," Caesar said with a laugh.

Kestrel stroked his hand over Zara's back. She fidgeted in his chair several times as if she was fighting herself to stay seated and not jump on him. He pressed his lips to the crook of her neck and kissed her sweet skin before whispering in her ear. "It's okay to run to Daddy."

Instantly, she bolted up from her chair to throw her arms around him. Kestrel lifted her off her feet as he kissed her lips hard. When he pulled back to look at her, he watched her blush enchantingly. "Come sit on Daddy's lap," he said quietly and scooped his arm under her knees before lowering them carefully to the seat.

Kestrel held her close and felt his heart lurch in his chest when she kissed his cheek before leaning back against his chest. "I like the hairdo," he complimented before looking at Sadie and Celeste.

"Did you all play beauty shop?"

"We did," Sadie crowed proudly and showed off her pink nails with blue polka dots.

Celeste lifted one foot from the ground to waggle the toe of her sensible lab shoes. "You can't see them, but I have lightning bolts on my toes."

"I don't ever do my nails," Zara shared. "I'm allergic to the chemicals in most polish. It makes me itch."

"That doesn't sound pleasant," Kestrel said, his eyebrows pulling together in concern.

"That's okay. You don't do yours either, do you, Daddy?"

Hawking snorted at the idea and then waggled a finger at Celeste when a scheming expression appeared on her face. "Don't even think about it."

Sadie immediately looked at Rocco, and he held up his hands. "Remember, rock climber, here. The polish would last three seconds." Sadie nodded sadly.

"We tried to talk Magnus into letting us paint his nails, but he was *busy*," Sadie shared, putting air quotes around that last word.

"I think I'll wait until my Little arrives to paint my fingernails. Besides, I *was* busy. Let's talk after dinner about what I found," Magnus suggested.

Kestrel nodded, not wishing to upset the Littles. Magnus would have shared the information right then if there was nothing concerning.

To distract everyone, he quickly asked Zara, "What did you do today?"

"I spliced some genes together. It was super cool."

"J-e-a-n-s or g-e-n-e-s?" he asked, spelling each word out.

"The G one, of course!"

"Sounds like Celeste is ready to make her next big discovery," Kestrel said.

"We're working hard to explore a variety of components to target. Zara came up with her theory, and we're testing it. It has potential," Celeste shared.

"You're being too kind. I'm learning so much. It's a thrill to work in the lab with a scientist who thinks concretely but outside the box," Zara said enthusiastically.

"We're a good pair," Celeste agreed.

Sadie smiled. "Meanwhile, up at the front desk, it's getting busier all the time. We had three empty rooms and sold out of all three when people without reservations appeared. There was even one guy I couldn't find a room for after that who wasn't too happy with me," Sadie informed them.

"You remember that panic button," Rocco warned with a concerned look.

"I won't forget. He left quickly after verifying that we have a room opening up tomorrow."

Kestrel shook his head. "You mentioned that people arrived without reservations yesterday, too. This concerns me. Is this a new trend or does it happen often?"

"Hmm. Not too often," Sadie confirmed. "More in the last week."

"Since I got here?" Zara squeaked.

"Yes," Sadie said, screwing up her mouth in concern as the pieces started falling in place.

"New rule," Kestrel said. "There are no rooms available for men arriving by themselves without reservations."

"Can we do that?" Sadie asked.

"Won't they just go online and make a reservation before coming to check in?" Celeste asked.

"She's right. They'll find a way to get around any rule we come up with. Or just come hang out in the lobby. We can't strongarm all the guests and visitors to screen out who we don't want here," Hawking pointed out.

"I'll just be very careful in case someone has figured out where I am," Zara said.

"The problem is that we don't know if these are the same traffickers from Mexico or new ones who saw you as you came through the airport," Phoenix pointed out.

"They're like cockroaches showing up everywhere," Zara said in disbelief.

"We don't know they're after you...yet." When a ding sounded almost underlining his words, Magnus turned to look at the screens in the computer area. Instead of results popping in from one of his searches, a picture of a food tray appeared.

"Dinner's ready. I'll go get it." Phoenix stood and walked to the elevator.

He returned a few minutes later with a laden cart filled with dishes that smelled divine. Covered dinner plates were stacked on the top. "I'm just going to circle the table and deliver these. They're hot, so they gave me gloves."

"It's a good thing we sent the fire expert," Caesar joked.

Phoenix waved his gloved hands before starting around the table. He set a plate down in front of Magnus and waited.

It took a few seconds for Magnus to realize he hadn't moved on. "You're killing me here. There's no spoon, so now we have a talking dish instead?"

"Oh, I forgot! I took care of that. We have a backup," Phoenix tried to pick up something from between the covered plates. His gloves made the act awkward, creating a problem.

"I can help," Sadie offered. When she saw what was on

the cart, she giggled and bumped her shoulder into Phoenix's broad one. Lifting it into the air, she held the serving spoon out to Magnus with a flourish.

"The kitchen staff was glad to send one down for us. They said we could keep it here," Phoenix explained.

"Well, at least our food won't get cold," Magnus commented, accepting the spoon. He launched into his activities of the day, giving Kestrel the impression he was coating over the things he'd found out about the men showing up without reservations and the helicopter guy.

After Magnus passed the spoon on, Kestrel stared at Magnus until the other man met his eyes from under that shielding baseball cap he seemed to live in. Seeing Magnus's infinitesimally brief nod, Kestrel knew there was more.

Chapter Twelve

Zara watched the men gathered around the tech center and stewed. Something was going on, and they weren't sharing. She knew it had to be about her. Every second that went by, she got angrier.

"I have every right to know what they're talking about, right?" she demanded of Sadie and Celeste as they watched a television program none of them were interested in.

"Yes," the two women agreed without hesitation.

Pushing herself to her feet, Zara tried to calm her suddenly speeding heart rate as she stomped over to the clump of men. "What's going on?" she said, her tone a little belligerent.

"Little girl, you need to watch your tone," Kestrel said with a frown.

"And you need to watch keeping me in the dark. This is my life. I get to know what's happening and at least help make some decisions," Zara said, trying to look brave as she made her demands.

Kestrel looked at her and nodded. "Not the best way to ask for information, Little girl, but I understand you're scared and concerned. I'm just trying to protect you, but you're right. You get to know what's going on."

"The guys arriving are coming from various countries. It's almost as if they were called here. I found this picture buried deep in the dark web," Magnus shared and switched a picture from his phone to one of the large screens above the computer system.

Gasps erupted from Sadie and Celeste. It was a photo of Zara holding a large sheet to detangle it. The wet fabric had soaked her shirt, and the normally baggy T-shirt material clung to her body. Obviously alone in the laundry area, she looked up to free a snarl above her head and smiled enchantingly.

Zara's heart sank. The picture was a trafficker's dream. It showed her natural beauty, unenhanced by makeup. The wet fabric drew everyone's eyes to her youthful, lush body. It also showed her working hard, proving her strength and resilience. Even she could see that some scumbag could want her for several illegal purposes.

"How did someone get that picture? It's from the laundry room here."

"I don't have a camera filming from that angle. The resort also doesn't have lenses like those. I went to check it out and found this."

Magnus pulled a small device from a drawer and placed it on the desk. "It had been carefully placed, so it was almost undetectable. I had to know the angle the picture was taken from to search for it."

"Were there other pictures on it?" she asked.

"It uploads immediately to a different site." Magnus flipped it over to show her the charred backside. "It ignited when I pulled it off the wall. I can't trace where the data went."

"Fingerprints?" Sadie asked.

"None. It was wiped clean, or they wore gloves. There was a hint of bleach residue. I'm not sure if that came from a cleaner used in the laundry room or from the person who installed it," Magnus explained.

Zara wrapped her arms around herself. She'd thought she'd been so careful. The idea that cameras had been watching her made her skin crawl.

Kestrel pulled her close to his body heat. "We're all here to keep you safe, Zara. They can't get to you without coming through us. I'm not going to let anything happen."

"It was interesting that as I came out of the laundry area, I ran into the laundry supervisor. Thankfully, he didn't seem to notice the device I held. He did ask where Zara had been reassigned. I faked a message coming in that got me out of there."

"Have you found anything new regarding our influx of single male guests?" Kestrel asked, refocusing their attention on the pressing matter at hand.

"I've investigated the men arriving. Two of the three most recent arrivals have ties to Asia. One to the Middle East. It's possible they'll give up if Zara isn't seen around the resort. They may think she's moved on," Magnus suggested.

"Here's what we've planned to do," Kestrel said as if knowing she needed to have a plan in place. "We're going to continue to keep you out of sight. Sadie, you could help us with the next step. Could you drop into different conversations that Zara asked for your help to get a work visa at a different resort and has moved to the north island to be closer to a friend who works there?"

"Oh, I can do that easily," Sadie agreed. "Anyone I should tell in particular?"

"It's probably best if you add it in whenever it fits the conversation. The rumor mill will spread it around," Rocco said.

"What about meals? The kitchen knows how many individual plates to send down. Someone paying attention would realize that six men plus Celeste and Sadie don't equal nine plates," Phoenix pointed out.

"We could order things like pizza that doesn't have a specific number of servings," Celeste suggested.

"Good idea. Daddies and Littles can share plates and glasses as well," Kestrel pointed out. "Then no one in the kitchen can track the number dining here."

"I am causing so much trouble. You could just help me get to the north island," Zara murmured, widening her eyes to keep the tears at bay. She didn't think she'd survive leaving her Daddy.

"You're not going anywhere, Little girl."

"No way," Celeste agreed. "If the guys had let Sadie and I leave because we were causing them problems, Sadie and I would've been stuck on a bus going anywhere but here. They want us here—no matter how much trouble we cause them. And we want you here, too."

"We're a team, Zara. Your Daddy will never let you go, and we won't ever let anyone hurt you," Caesar told her firmly.

Nodding, Zara looked at each of their faces before saying, "Thank you. I don't know how I'll ever repay you."

"No repayment needed, Little Swan," Kestrel told her.

Celeste's eyes widened. "Little Swan? I love that. It's so you. Regal but fierce. I got attacked by a swan at the lake one time. They're vicious if they think you're going to endanger their babies. I just wanted to pet the fluff on one's head." When Hawking looked at her and shook his head, she protested. "What? I was like six. And it all stuck up like this!" Celeste thrust her fingers into the air on top of her head.

"I'd want to pet that," Sadie said, nodding. Then she added, "Now that we know what's going on, let's leave the men to their discussions." She turned toward Zara. "You need a swan on your door."

"I noticed both of yours. I don't know that I can draw a swan," Zara said sadly.

"I think there's one in my coloring book. Let's go look!" Celeste said, grabbing Zara's and Sadie's hands to head for the small art area set up at the side of the room.

They were embroiled in decorating animal pictures when Kestrel dropped a kiss on Zara's hair before pulling out the chair next to his Little girl and sitting down. After spreading a protective sheet of heavy paper on the table, Kestrel opened a tackle box and pulled out three rocks with a base coat already covering them. Choosing a paintbrush and opening a few paint jars, he decorated the rocks. One became a penguin on a floating ice island, another a black cat sitting in front of the moon, and the third, a beautiful swan on a lake.

The three women watched him carefully, and each exclaimed their delight as the designs came together to form their favorites. Having been warned, they didn't dare touch them in case they smudged the paint as it dried.

"What are you going to do with them?" Zara asked.

"I usually place these around the resort for fun. People love to find them," Kestrel explained. "I think maybe these special ones might want to stay with you three—when they're dry, of course."

"I'd love that," Zara confessed. "Could you teach me? I'd love to make people smile."

"That sounds like a perfect project for a rainy, windy day when I can't fly the helicopter," Kestrel suggested.

"A couple of those coming up, I'm afraid," Magnus murmured.

"He doesn't miss anything, does he?" Zara asked before yawning.

"Time for bed, Little girl. Say goodnight to your friends," Kestrel instructed.

"Can I put my swan up before bed?" Zara asked, holding up the swan picture she had decorated.

"I think we can steal a few minutes to do that first," Kestrel allowed as they cleaned up the area while leaving the rocks to dry completely.

When they were finished, Zara hugged Celeste and Sadie goodnight before slipping her hand into Kestrel's. "I'm ready, Daddy."

She loved his smile. No one was as handsome as her Daddy. Yes, all the guys were buff and physically fit. Yes, they were all good-looking, but her Daddy was *it* for her. Zara was sure Celeste and Sadie thought their Daddies were incredible, too, and that made her happy. She wanted her friends to be with someone who made their hearts race—just like hers did.

Zara squeezed Kestrel's hand as they rode the elevator silently.

"You okay, Little Swan?" he asked, his brows drawing together in concern.

"I'm scared, but I feel safe with you and the others."

"I'm glad." He ushered her out as the doors opened.

"Do you have any tape?" she asked.

"Of course. It's right here," Kestrel said, opening a drawer in one of the end tables in the front gathering area and waving it.

"Yay! Let's put my picture on our door."

She rushed forward to hold the swan on the door. "Here or here?" she asked, pressing it higher and lower. Zara looked over her shoulder at the other doors to see where Celeste and Sadie had placed theirs.

"How about the middle?" Kestrel proposed.

"Good idea, Daddy. Then we can both see it well."

She held it carefully in place as Kestrel rolled the tape into loops. He put one on the backside at each corner to hold it securely and invisibly. Zara stepped back and clapped. It looked perfect. Her door wasn't empty anymore.

My door?

Zara looked up at the handsome man who watched her. It really was her door. She'd come here all alone and so scared. She was still afraid, but it was different now, knowing she wasn't alone. Kestrel would do anything to keep her safe. More important than that, he'd made a life and home for her. Working with Celeste and sharing time with the team made every day better. Zara rushed forward to wrap her arms around Kestrel's waist.

"Thank you," she whispered.

"You're welcome, Zara. I'm glad to help hang your picture. I'm happier to have you here with me," Kestrel assured her.

"I'm happiest to be here, too. Could you do me a favor?"

"Probably...? But I'm not going to take you for a helicopter ride for a while." He looked at her cautiously. "Is there something else you'd like me to do?"

"Make love to me, Daddy?"

"That I can very definitely do." Kestrel smiled as he

walked forward. Leaning over, he wrapped his arms around her waist and draped her over his shoulder.

As he carried her inside, the elevator dinged, and Hawking and Celeste emerged. Zara waved to her friend and then grinned when Celeste gave her a thumbs up.

Chapter Thirteen

Kestrel carried her straight to the large bed she already loved to sleep in. Leaning over, he lowered her bottom to the mattress, then plucked Coco from his place on the pillow.

"Coco isn't old enough to see what I plan to do to you. I'll set him on the dresser," Kestrel told her as he walked away.

"Um," Zara protested when he set the monkey down, facing them. She twirled her finger, and he nodded.

"Good idea."

When Coco faced the wall, Kestrel walked slowly toward her. Reaching over his shoulder in a delicious display of muscles, he pulled his Danger Bluff polo over his head and tossed it to the side. His focus rested squarely on her.

Zara sat up to take her shirt off and froze at his, "No way, Little girl. I get to unwrap my present myself."

"Present?" she squeaked.

"Oh, very definitely," Kestrel assured her as he unfastened his pants and pushed his slacks over his hips and down to the floor. Stepping out of his shoes, he leaned forward to tug off his socks without ever losing eye contact with her. He stalked forward in his tight boxer briefs that left nothing to her imagination.

Kestrel rested one knee on the bed as he brushed her hands away from the hem of her shirt. He pulled it slowly over her head. Zara could feel his gaze roaming over her skin. He'd seen her naked repeatedly, but she understood that, this time, he would make her his completely.

He smiled as he lowered his gaze to her chest, and his smile broadened as he used one finger to trail along the edge of her lacy bra. "I love this blue. It makes your eyes pop. How many sets of sexy lingerie do you own, Little girl?"

"A lot. I guess bra-and-panty sets are my guilty pleasure."

"Not complaining." He dipped his head and nuzzled between her breasts before dragging his tongue along the edge of the lace.

Zara grabbed his waist and arched her chest as a soft moan escaped her mouth. Every time he touched her, it felt so good. She came alive. It felt like she'd known him much longer than reality. And the way he looked at her...

She couldn't quite describe how his gaze lit her on fire. It was reverent and filled with deep sincerity. He never looked at her like every man she'd seen in her life. His look didn't make her feel objectified.

When his tongue slid under the edge of the lace to flick her nipple, she whimpered. "Daddy..."

He rose onto his knees and held her gaze while he unbuttoned her jeans before dragging them and her shoes off her body.

His grin widened as he hovered once more, his gaze locked on the matching panties. With his usual reverence, he trailed a finger across her stomach just above the lace. "Your skin... It's so soft."

Curiosity made her slide her palms up his chest while she

asked, "You said sleeping with me would be a first for you, too. Surely you didn't mean..." She let her voice trail off, words failing her.

He gave her a sweet kiss. "I meant that I've never had sex with anyone other than in a casual relationship. Never with anyone I knew was my Little girl. Never with anyone I knew I wanted to spend the rest of my life with. I had girlfriends and a few partners when I was younger, but it's been a very long time since I've taken a woman to my bed."

"But why? You're so sexy and...well, perfect."

He grinned. "I'm far from perfect, Little Swan. If you asked any of my recent girlfriends, they would tell you I was too nice."

"Too nice?" Her voice lifted. "How is that a thing?" She had so little experience with men. She suddenly wished she'd at least had close girlfriends who would have filled in some of the holes in her knowledge. She'd never even participated in the kind of banter she knew girls whispered among themselves.

Kestrel continued to stroke her skin with a fingertip while he spoke. "Women see me—the muscles, the tattoos, and my size—and expect me to be Dominant. And I am. I'm extremely Dominant but not in the way they expect."

Zara shivered. He was certainly Dominant. She'd seen evidence of that firsthand several times. He could dominate her with just a look. She was almost afraid to ask. "What do they expect?"

He shrugged. "Someone rougher. Bossier. Someone who might make them get on their knees and hold their hair while demanding a blow job."

Her breath hitched. She suddenly pictured herself on her knees in front of him, staring up at him. The idea didn't turn her off, but she couldn't picture Kestrel demanding such a thing.

He leaned in and kissed her lips gently before rising above her. "Little Swan, you're killing me with your eyes."

"Their color?"

He shook his head. "No, Little girl. It's what I can see behind them. I sparked your curiosity. Don't get me wrong. If you ever feel like taking my cock into your mouth, I won't stop you, but the choice will always be yours. Because, see... I'm nice," he teased.

She knew exactly what he meant as his finger trailed up between her breasts. She could visualize his hand gently sliding through her hair, his gaze hazy with lust, and his erection rock-hard as he forced himself to stay still for her to explore. If that's what he meant by being a nice guy, she wouldn't complain.

"So, you haven't had sex with anyone recently?" She was still probing for information to help her understand.

He shook his head. "I hate to compare what I've dealt with to what you've faced. There is no comparison. But there are similarities. Any time I walked into a bar or club, women swarmed me. Most of them just wanted a notch in their bedpost, the bragging rights that they'd slept with someone in uniform."

She chuckled. "So, you felt objectified like me."

"Yes, but like I said, no comparison. I would never make light of your situation. I'm significantly larger, and I could take someone down with one hand if I needed to. Being objectified as a man means shrugging off pawing women when they try to rub against me. I'm well aware it's far scarier if you're the woman on the receiving end of unwanted attention. And, Zara, I'm so sorry you've had to deal with that all these years. I'm sure it's unnerving and maddening at best, scary and unsafe at other times."

She gave a slow nod. He understood.

He drew in a breath. "The truth is, I realized years ago that having sex with women who didn't mean anything to me was a waste of my time. Once I understood I was a Daddy, I knew I would wait until I found the perfect Little girl before I took someone else to my bed. Until now, I had never met her. None of them were you."

Her heart rate picked up the pace as he held her gaze with every bit of sincerity.

"It's happening so fast," she murmured.

"It feels right, and I know you feel it, too. But, Little Swan, I would never pressure you. If you're not ready, we won't have sex." His voice was strong. His gaze insistent.

"Because you're nice."

One corner of his lips lifted in a half-smile. "Because I'm nice, Little girl."

"Well, it turns out I like nice guys." She spread her fingers and let them glide all over his chest, learning his hard lines and edges, the way his muscles flexed under her touch. When she slid the tips of her fingers over the tattoo under his left arm, she leaned in closer to read it. "What does it say, Daddy?"

He glanced down at the words. "God grant me the serenity to accept things I cannot change, courage to change things I can, and wisdom to know the difference."

"That's so...nice," she whispered, unable to come up with something else.

He chuckled. "See? Nice." He dropped his hands on either side of her and leaned in closer. "It's pretty applicable, I think. We've had a tough road to get to each other. I wouldn't change the path that brought me to you. Now that we're together, we'll make our own future. I'm smart enough to know this is the real deal. I'm yours, Little Swan. And you're mine."

She smiled. Her heart felt so full. "I guess there's no denying it. We should probably accept the truth and make it official."

He leaned over to kiss her. "If you're ready, Little Swan," he murmured against her lips.

"I'm ready, Daddy." Her life was upside down and inside out right now. She was on the run from human traffickers. There was no guarantee she would ever be safe. She couldn't predict the future. But, for now, for today, she felt the safest she'd felt in many years. She was in her Daddy's arms. It felt right. No matter what happened tomorrow or the next day or next week or next year, she wanted Kestrel to have claimed her virginity this night.

Kestrel rose again and opened the front clasp of her bra, letting her heavy breasts free. After sliding the straps down her arms and tugging the lace out from under her, he shifted down and pulled her panties off, too.

Breathing heavily, she watched as he rose from the bed, took off his own underwear, and then snagged a box from the nightstand. He cursed under his breath as he removed the cellophane wrapper. "I should've done this earlier," he apologized.

She disagreed. She enjoyed watching him struggle. For one thing, she liked knowing he had that unopened box in his drawer. It said a lot about him. He'd been prepared, but not quite ready. Plus, the slight fluster made her feel cherished and important.

He finally held up a condom triumphantly.

She giggled. "You don't really need that, Daddy," she finally told him.

He lifted both brows.

She shrugged. "I mean, I assume you've been tested since the last time you were with someone; I'm certainly clean, and I've taken birth control for years to regulate my periods."

He stood frozen for a moment before licking his lips. "You sure?"

She nodded and reached for him.

He dropped the box and the loose condom in the open drawer and climbed back over her. "With a condom on, I might've lasted fifteen seconds. Without a condom, I'll last five seconds."

She ran her hands up his back as he settled between her legs. "I bet we could do it twice," she proposed, feeling bold.

"I bet we could do it five times," he countered. He lowered his mouth to her neck and kissed a path to her ear. "Once I've been inside you, I'm never going to want to pull out."

She tipped her head to the side to give him better access. "I'm never going to want you to pull out."

Kestrel brought his mouth to hers, settled his elbows alongside her head, and cupped her face before taking her lips in a heated kiss that made her toes curl. She was moaning into his mouth in seconds. Then she started squirming as her body made its demands. Wetness welled from her core. His cock grew harder and harder where it was lodged against her sex, but he didn't move.

"Daddy..." she whined when he finally released her lips.

"Let me take my time, Little Swan," he murmured as he slid down the bed, kissing a path between her breasts.

She whimpered at the loss of his hard length against her, but then her breath hitched as he took one of her nipples into his mouth and twirled his tongue around and around the tip.

Her eyes rolled back and her mouth fell open, but before

she could form thoughts or words, he was moving again, kissing a path down her stomach until he reached her sex.

If she'd had the ability to react, she would have been embarrassed and pushed him away, but there wasn't time. His lips were wrapped around her clit, his tongue flicking the swollen gland as he moaned against her.

"Oh God... Daddy..." A pressure was building and building—so fast she couldn't stop it. It was the same thing that had happened the night before when he'd given her an orgasm in the tub.

Zara bucked her hips against his mouth. It felt so good. She couldn't believe he had his mouth on her *there*, but she wasn't going to complain. He was humming as though he enjoyed it.

Kestrel gripped her inner thighs, parted her folds, and slid a thumb up inside her.

That was all it took for her to tip over the edge, and then she was falling as pulsing waves of her release consumed her. She might have been moaning, too. She wasn't sure. All her focus was on how good it felt. If it was always going to be like this, she would never leave the bedroom.

When her Daddy finally lifted his head, he was grinning. He wiped his mouth on the sheet and then crawled up her body until his erection was once again lodged at her entrance.

Zara was panting, unable to catch her breath. "Will it always be like that?"

"Nope. It will get better." He kissed her, sharing her flavor.

A shudder shook her body as she tasted herself for the first time. Salty and sweet. She supposed she tasted like sex.

Breaking free of his lips, she wiggled. "Need you inside me, Daddy."

He cupped her face. "You're sure, Little Swan?"

She nodded. "Please, Daddy..."

He dragged his length along her folds, making her gasp as the exposed nerve endings came back to life. His brow furrowed as he met her gaze. "I'll go slow, Little one, but it's going to be tight this first time."

She grabbed his butt cheeks with her hands, digging her blunt nails into his firm flesh. "I'll be fine. Make love to me, Kestrel."

As if their bodies were meant to be aligned, he didn't even reach between them to line his shaft up with her entrance. It seemed to know where to go on its own.

Kestrel held her gaze as he eased into her.

Zara gasped at the intense pressure. She was nervous. She'd heard it would hurt. But he was right there with her, and the slight twinge wasn't as bad as she'd expected. Mostly, she felt stretched.

"More, Little one?"

She nodded, not breathing.

Kestrel continued, slowly filling her until her eyes rolled back, and all she could do was wait for the pressure to pass.

"Breathe, Zara."

She nodded quickly but didn't do as he asked.

He lowered his face until his lips hovered above hers. "Breathe for me, Little Swan."

She forced her mouth to open, drew a long breath, and let it back out.

"Am I hurting you?"

She shook her head.

"Words, Little Swan."

"It's just tight," she whispered, "but..."

"But what, Zara?"

"I think I need you to move now."

His responding moan made her body come alive. He eased partway out and then thrust back in deeper this time.

It felt...good. So very good.

He did it again.

She moaned as he slid almost out and then thrust in with more force. She gripped his butt cheeks again. Now, it felt even better. "Again, Daddy."

Kestrel brought his lips to hers and kissed her deeply. He wasn't moving any other muscle, and a growing need blossomed and took over until she was writhing beneath him.

When he released her lips and lifted his face a few inches, she panted. "More, Daddy."

A long, low moan rumbled through him as he picked up the pace. Sliding into her over and over again, he varied his strokes as if experimenting. Zara enjoyed everything until —*there!*

Her gasp brought his gaze to meet hers. "Do it again," she begged, clinging to his muscular shoulders as she wrapped her legs around him.

"Zara," he breathed as he surged deeper inside her.

He was the rock that supported her as all the emotions crashed through her body. Her gaze fixed on her handsome Daddy, and she knew the control he battled to lavish her with pleasure. His face was tight, but his eyes were rolled back now.

Suddenly, he lifted one hip and wiggled a hand between their bodies, confusing her for a moment until his fingers found her clit. The moment he pressed against it, her entire body convulsed in another orgasm.

This one was so different because her channel gripped at his shaft, pulsing around it, making the climax so much more intense and deep. She curled her fingers in reaction, feeling her nails bite into his skin.

On a long groan, Kestrel held himself fully seated. She knew by his stiff posture and the way his body twitched over and over that his orgasm was following hers. A feeling of power and excitement filled her. She could tantalize her Daddy as much as he could her.

She loved watching him as he slowly came back to her. His expressions matched the way she felt, and she started running her hands up and down his back. Leaning forward to press kisses on his damp skin, she savored his warm scent.

When his gaze met hers, he smiled. "Am I hurting you, Little Swan?"

She shook her head.

"Want me to pull out?"

"No, Daddy. Stay right there for a few minutes. I like it. I feel...connected to you."

He brought his lips to hers for a long, sweet kiss. "God, you feel good."

"When can we do it again?"

Chapter Fourteen

Kestrel chuckled at his eager Little girl as he eased out of her, watching her face closely to make sure she didn't wince. If she did, it would affect his answer.

She whimpered at the loss but showed no signs of being in pain. She even pushed her cute bottom lip out. "Why'd you do that?"

He kissed her breasts one at a time as he moved to stand. "As much as I'd love to stay inside you in theory, it's not particularly practical. Don't move," he ordered as he padded to the bathroom.

He snagged two washcloths and wet both with warm water. Taking a second, he used one on himself, tossed it into the hamper, and returned to his Little girl with the other one.

Zara was right where he'd left her, but as he approached, she grew modest and pulled her legs together.

"Uh-huh, Little girl. Let Daddy clean you up and examine you."

She gasped. "I can do it." She reached for the cloth he held.

He gave her a narrow-eyed look. "I will always take care of you in every way, Little girl. Open your legs for me."

She sighed but relented and parted her knees wide. "So bossy," she told the ceiling.

He leaned close to examine her folds before gently wiping her clean. There was only a mild trace of blood. Any barrier she might have been born with had probably worked itself open from riding bikes or playing on the monkey bars.

"Nothing hurts?" He wanted clarification. "Don't lie to Daddy. That's the fastest way to end up over my knees with my palm on your cute bottom."

She lifted her head, eyes wide. "You would really spank me?"

"In a heartbeat."

"What if I don't want you to spank me?" She trembled as she asked. She also drew her knees closer together.

"Then, after the first time, you'll either decide not to disobey Daddy, or we'll come up with other forms of discipline."

"What other forms of discipline?" She licked her lips, her body trembling.

He pushed her thighs open wider and kissed her pussy. "Whatever form makes you squirm, Little Swan."

Her breath hitched. "Why would I squirm while you were punishing me?"

"For the same reason you're squirming right now, Little one. It's pretty common for Little girls to enjoy being disciplined. It feels good. It purges the naughty behavior or any other worrisome thoughts you might be having."

She stared at him. "I don't get it."

He smiled as he crawled up next to her and dropped onto one side, pulling her close and cupping her face. "You will."

She sat upright and twisted to look at him. "Show me."

"Now?" He was surprised she had the energy to bolt up like she had. Did she really want him to spank her?

"Yes. You said I would ask you when I was ready. I'm ready."

He remained on his side, trailing a finger up her arm. Fuck, she was gorgeous. He had no idea how to tell her that out loud without sounding like every other asshole on earth who had ogled her and objectified her, so he kept his thoughts to himself. But, damn, she was even sexier right now than at any prior moment since he'd laid eyes on her.

Back straight, hair flowing all around her, swollen lips, pinkened cheeks, high, full tits with rosy nipples... Just...damn.

She reached out and touched his face with a shaky finger. "Say it."

He jerked his gaze to hers. "Say what, Little Swan?"

"Say what you're thinking. I need to hear it. I know you're trying to be careful about becoming one of the thousands of men who have made me feel like an object all my life, but I don't feel like that when I'm with you. I feel cherished. I need to hear the words. I promise I won't freak out."

He slowly rose to sit next to her, scooted back to lean against the headboard, lifted her off the bed, and settled her on his lap, straddling him. Her warm pussy pressed against his still-hard erection, cradling it.

She cupped his face and pulled her shoulders back with confidence. And then she waited.

He licked his lips, wanting to say just the right things even though he didn't think he could go wrong with her. But this was important. She needed him to make her feel as desirable as she was.

"You are the most important person in my life, Zara, and you always will be. It wouldn't matter if you were fat or skinny, short or tall. I wouldn't care if you were bald, had scars, or grew a third arm."

She smiled warmly, playing with the short hair at the back of his head.

"Even if you were all those things at once, I would think you were the most stunning woman in the world because you're mine. Because what matters most—and mattered first —is what's in here." He tapped her temple. "And here..." He trailed his finger down to her heart.

She giggled. "I can't be both fat and skinny, short and tall, Daddy."

He chuckled, making them both shake. "You're perfect, Zara. So unbelievably perfect. Rocco feels the same way about Sadie, and Hawking feels the same way about Celeste. I don't care that the whole world thinks you're the ideal woman. You're *my* woman. My Little girl. You bring me to my knees, and you will even when you're old and gray."

He was so close to telling her he loved her, but that felt too soon. The words hovered there between them. *I love you so much it hurts, Zara.*

She threw her arms around him and hugged him tight. "Thank you, Daddy. You're perfect, too."

He slid his arms around her slender body and pulled her even closer. His cock twitched against her.

When she finally released him and leaned back, she said, "Now, will you spank me? Then you'll know if you also like it when my skin is red."

He chuckled at her joke. "Oh, sweet Little Swan, my cock will get two times harder if I pinken your bottom with my palm."

She shuddered delightfully. "That's pretty big, Daddy. I think I need to see it," she teased.

"You're sure?" Was this really the right time to spank her? They were in a state of post-coital bliss. He didn't want to ruin that, but he also wanted to give her what she needed when she asked for it.

"Okay, Little Swan, but I have a rule, and I expect you to obey it." He lifted a brow to make sure he had her attention.

"What rule, Daddy?" she asked before biting her full, sexy bottom lip.

"You must always be honest with Daddy about how my discipline makes you feel. If you don't like it, you need to tell me. Some Little girls really don't like being spanked. It's not a mandatory part of our dynamic."

"But Sadie and Celeste like it."

"Yes, they both do. It's a pretty common facet of age play. I'd say most Little girls enjoy the release they get from a hard spanking. But not all. Understand?"

"Yes, Daddy."

"And you'll stop me if you aren't feeling it?"

"Yes, Daddy."

"Good girl." He lifted her off his lap. "Come around to the side and lie over my lap, Little Swan."

It was adorable the way she crawled to one side and then lowered herself over his thighs.

He reached for her wrists and drew them to the small of her back, where he gripped them together with one hand.

Her breath hitched at that simple action, and she squeezed her thighs together. Yeah, the chances of her not enjoying a spanking were slim.

"Part your legs, Zara."

She shivered, but she did as she was told.

He set his palm on her bottom, watching as goosebumps rose all over her body. "My Little girl is so very curious."

"Yes, Daddy." Her voice was breathy, and when she lifted her head to arch her back, her breasts swayed against his thigh, making his cock stiffen harder than ever.

"Lie down, Little Swan. Relax your body." That was a tall order, but she managed to set her cheek on the mattress and even let go of the tightness in her bottom. "Good girl."

He lifted his palm and delivered a gentle swat.

She flinched ever so slightly but had no other reaction.

He did it again several more times, switching back and forth between her cheeks, keeping his gaze on her face.

When he stopped to rub her bottom and take her pulse, she lifted her head, twisted it around, and frowned at him. "*That's* a spanking?" Her voice was incredulous.

He chuckled. "Okay then, naughty girl. You ready now?"

She rolled her eyes as she let herself recline again.

It was hard not to laugh. Maybe she would be fine with enduring a good, hard spanking. When he resumed, he swatted her harder. Hard enough to get her attention. Hard enough to leave the faint outline of his hand on her bottom.

This time, she flinched, but a second later, she sighed as though relieved.

Kestrel gave her half a dozen swats before he paused again to check with her. "Better?"

She nodded, not lifting her head this time. Her body was limp. Sated. He hadn't thought Littles could so easily accept a spanking without stiffening and remaining nervous throughout the first experience.

Zara continued to shock and surprise him, though. She was so strong and determined. Even though she'd been skeptical and had her doubts, she was in a zone now.

"More?"

"Yes, Daddy." Her voice was soft and submissive.

He spanked her again, covering her entire bottom until it was bright red before he shifted his attention to the backs of her thighs. When he struck the sweet spot right at the base of her bottom, her heels lifted into the air, her thighs stiffened, and she moaned.

Damn, she was responsive and so fucking sexy.

He continued, not wanting to go too much harder but wanting her to get the full experience. When she clenched her butt cheeks, he stopped spanking her, reached between her legs, and stroked through her folds.

Zara squealed as she clenched his hand with her inner thighs.

Fuck, she was so wet and swollen. She lifted her head off the bed and moaned. "Daddy..."

This was not a punishment spanking. It had been an introduction. An experiment. He would reward her. After finding her clit and swirling around it, he thrust two fingers into her tight warmth.

Zara moaned so loudly the sound reverberated through his own body, especially his cock. "Oh God..."

He pressed his thumb against her clit and thrust his other three fingers into her, stretching her channel, driving her higher and higher until she came so hard that her pussy gripped his fingers.

She went rigid; her body arched.

He waited until she shuddered at the end of her release to ease his fingers out of her and pull back. He brought them to his mouth and sucked her essence from each finger while she dropped back down, limp over his lap, panting.

Kestrel gave her bottom a final pat and then gently rolled her over so he could cradle her in his arms.

She blinked up at him, punch drunk from either the

spanking or the orgasm or both. She was smiling, and her eyes were glazed over. "I get it now."

He returned the grin. "If I gave you ten rules to live by tomorrow, how many of them would you break before lunch?"

She smiled wider. "All of them, Daddy."

Chapter Fifteen

It was only the second night sleeping with her Daddy, but Zara felt at home, snuggled in his arms. Her bottom was warm and tingly. Her heart was still beating fast. Her mind was settling.

Her vision of making love several times in a row had been obliterated. She was too sated and relaxed to have sex again tonight, but she wanted to be sure he knew she was going to want to do that again as soon as she woke up.

"Did you set an alarm, Daddy?" she mumbled.

"No, Little Swan. There's no need for you to get up early. You're still behind on your sleep. I want you to rest and make your way downstairs to the basement refreshed. I don't care if it's ten in the morning. I'll let Celeste know."

She twisted her head around to look at him from her spooned position. He'd turned off all the lights, but being the amazing Daddy he was, he'd put a night light on next to the bathroom. So thoughtful.

The dim light was enough to see his face. "I wasn't

thinking of my work schedule, Daddy. I was thinking of yours. What time is your first appointment?"

He kissed her cheek. "Nine. Not too early."

"Then set the alarm for eight please." She settled back down in his embrace.

"Why would I do that, Little Swan? I'll wake up in plenty of time to make a nine o'clock appointment."

"Like you did today?" she teased. "You only had nine minutes to make it to the helipad."

He gave her a squeeze, but he also tickled her under her breast. "Naughty girl. Today was an odd exception. It won't happen again, I promise. You don't have to worry about Daddy making it to work on time."

She twisted again. "Daddy, I'm not worried about you making it to the helipad. I'm just saying nine minutes isn't enough time for us to have sex before you leave, and I want to wake up to the feel of your hard erection pressing into me."

He chuckled as he cupped her breast. "Is that a fantasy of yours, Little Swan?" He flicked her nipple.

She gasped and arched into his palm. "Yes. It happens in all the books and movies. The man wakes up first. He stares down at the heroine for a while, smiling, admiring her beauty, and thinking about how lucky he is, and then he pushes her leg forward and eases into her before she's awake," she declared. Duh, everyone knew that.

His laughter filled the room. "I don't think real life is quite as glamorous." His hand slid down from her breast to her sex while he used his knee to push her top leg up high. After lifting his hand around to stroke through her wet folds, he whispered into her ear. "Do you honestly think you could sleep through something like this and not wake up until I thrust into you?"

She shrugged, loving the feel of his lips on her ear. "So

far, you've hit all the highlights in any romance novel, Daddy. I think you can do that one, too."

He added a second finger and scissored them, stretching her and making her moan. "What if I just slide into you now and stay there all night? That way, I could just start moving in the morning to wake you up."

"That's a great idea," she responded.

He removed his fingers and dragged her wetness up her tummy and over her nipple. "Little Swan, that's not even realistic enough for a book. It couldn't happen in real life."

She pouted. "Hmph."

He chuckled again. God, he loved her. She was both strong and independent while maintaining the most adorable innocence at the same time. "Sleep, Little Swan. I'll be right here." He stroked her hair and watched her as she fully relaxed and eventually fell into a deep sleep.

He stayed awake for a long time, just staring at her. It wasn't her beauty that mesmerized him so much as the fact that she was his. She was here in his arms. He'd waited a lifetime to find his Little girl, and now he had her.

He tried not to think about the danger she was in and what challenges they might face, but it was impossible to ignore their problems. He truly didn't like the number of random single men registered at this hotel. Was he being paranoid? He didn't think so. How many single men went to a resort to vacation alone? There could be one or two, but not many more than that.

Kestrel was thinking ahead now. He needed to be sure his Little girl understood not to wander anywhere in the resort except the basement and the fifth floor, using only the designated elevator. That was the only way he knew to keep her safe.

They couldn't live like this forever. She'd go stir-crazy.

Even after only one day, he could see the effects in her eyes. She wasn't the sort of woman who would endure being cooped up, no matter how large the space was.

He needed to meet with the team tomorrow and get more proactive about the threat against her. It was mind-boggling why anyone would go to so much trouble to hunt down a woman on the other side of the earth in order to kidnap her and sell her.

If all these men staying at Danger Bluff Mountain Resort were in cahoots and angling to grab her, they must have a very fucking high bid.

Kestrel shuddered at the thought. *Fuck. Fuck fuck fuck.*

It reminded him of a drug dealer. If someone had a large amount of drugs, and they promised them to a buyer, and then they misplaced them and didn't show up for the exchange...

Is that what had happened here? Had someone already paid for Zara, and then the seller couldn't deliver? It was the most likely scenario under the circumstances. If several people were undercover at the resort, waiting for an opportunity to kidnap her, then someone was willing to go to any expense to get their hands on her.

How much did the world's prettiest woman go for?

Anger consumed Kestrel at the thought. No matter what the price was on her head, they would never get her. He would make sure of it.

Chapter Sixteen

Zara was dreaming. It was a very, very good dream, too. She was with the sexiest man she'd ever met, and he was making sweet love to her. In fact, his hands were holding her legs open as he eased his shaft in and out of her channel.

God, it felt so good. She didn't want to wake up. She prayed she would get to stay in the dream forever.

A moan startled her, and when she realized it was coming from her, she was yanked out of the dream. Or was she?

A slow smile spread across her face when she opened her eyes to find Kestrel's large hand holding her thigh up near her chest. He was inside her, easing slowly in and out.

"There she is," he murmured against her ear. "I guess the smutty parts of romance novels can be recreated."

She closed her eyes and luxuriated in the amazing feelings consuming her. Yeah...this was the best morning of her life.

Daddy slid his hand under her thigh to find her clit. As soon as he started rubbing it, she moaned.

"You must've been having a really good dream because

you were already writing against me when I reached between your legs," he informed her.

She couldn't remember. Or maybe she had been having a great sex dream when he'd taken over, giving her the real thing.

She liked this angle, with him behind her and rolling over her almost, pinning her to the mattress. She felt like she was in a cocoon, safe, protected, cherished. She could ignore all her problems.

"Come around my cock, Little Swan. I want to feel your pussy clench around me."

She moaned as his words slid around her like silk, his breath on her neck, his lips tasting behind her ear.

When his fingers sped up, she was lost. She came just as he'd demanded, her pussy clenching his shaft as he followed right behind her.

Minutes later, they were both panting, and her Daddy was still lodged inside her, having rolled even tighter against her. He moved his hand back to her thigh, right above her knee, pressing her into the mattress.

"I could get used to this," she whispered as she set her hand on top of his.

"Mmm. I'm already used to it. I think I'll wake you up like this every day." He kissed her neck again and rubbed his unshaven face gently against her sensitive skin. "Unfortunately, I have to get up and get in the shower."

"Can I come with you?" she asked eagerly.

"Little Swan, I will never turn down an offer to shower with you, but you're welcome to snuggle back under the covers and sleep a while longer if you want."

She shook her head. "I'd rather shower with you, Daddy."

She whimpered as he eased out of her, and when he gave her space, she rolled to her back and stared up at him. She was completely exposed, arms and legs spread open as if she didn't have a modest bone in her body.

It was a new feeling. She'd never trusted a living soul to see her like this before. She hadn't even liked it when people looked at her fully clothed. But as her Daddy stood by the side of the bed and looked down at her, she felt...pretty.

His lust was genuine. Desire poured from his expression. And she felt even sexier when he set a finger on her leg and trailed it up her body as if he were drawing her or memorizing her. When he reached her breast, he circled her nipple and continued on, leaving her panting and wanting again.

"Shower," he repeated, his voice gravelly. He snagged her hand and tugged. "And we don't have time for sex in the shower."

"Do we have more than nine minutes?" she teased.

He chuckled as he lifted her from the bed and tossed her over his shoulder. He swatted her bottom. "You'll never let me live that down, will you, naughty girl?"

"Nope." She grinned. Yeah, she would never be happier than she was right this moment.

Or so she thought until he set her on her feet under the warm spray of the shower and started running his soapy hands all over her body. Maybe this moment was even better.

Then he filled his palms with shampoo and gave her the best head massage of her life. That moment was even better.

When he finished washing the two of them and led her out of the shower, he dried her off with a fluffy towel, pulled on a pair of tight boxers, and sat her down in front of the mirror. As he picked up a comb and gently worked through the tangles in her hair, she closed her eyes, moaned, and knew she'd reached yet another perfect moment.

"If you don't stop making all those sexy noises, I'm going to miss my nine o'clock," he drawled.

"Hmm. I don't think I can help you out with that. Maybe you could tell them you overslept, or there was a fire in your apartment, or your girlfriend was naked in your arms..."

He leaned over her from behind, cupped her cheek, and kissed her nose. "I like the sound of that."

"What part? The fire?" she teased.

"The girlfriend. Though I'd prefer to call you my Little girl, for the vanilla world, we'll stick with girlfriend."

She twisted around and stood, bouncing on the balls of her feet. "So you'll do it? You'll tell them you couldn't make it?"

He took a step back and shook a finger at her. "You are a very naughty Little girl. Don't move."

She couldn't stop grinning as he left her standing in the bathroom. He was back two minutes later, fully dressed, holding up clothes for her.

She switched her smile to a pout. "Darn. You're going to go to work, aren't you?"

"Yes, and when I get a break, I'm going to give you your first punishment spanking for being so tempting and naughty this morning." He set her clothes on the counter, took the towel from her, hung it up, and grabbed her panties. Squatting down, he said, "Step in, Little Swan."

She grabbed his shoulders and lifted a leg, but she did so rocking toward him so that her pussy was closer to his face.

When he stood, he was shaking his head, but he was smiling at the same time. "I'm going to spank that little bottom of yours until it's bright red."

"But Daddy, that's not a punishment. I found out I like it when you spank me."

He chuckled. "Oh, Little Swan, that spanking I gave you last night wasn't a punishment spanking. It was the sensual kind. When you're naughty, you won't get to come afterward.

In fact, you'll go straight to the corner for a timeout until your arousal subsides."

She gasped. Would he do that? When he held up her matching pink bra, she pushed out her bottom lip. "No fun."

"That pout of yours is adorable, Little Swan. It's not going to cause you to win any arguments, though."

Darn. This being Little was not quite what she'd envisioned. Punishments? Timeouts? Withholding orgasms?

He pulled a dress over her head next. It wasn't one she'd ever seen before. "Where did this come from?" she asked. It was so feminine. A soft pink that made her skin glow. It fit her perfectly, snug around her breasts before flowing out around her from beneath them. It hung halfway down her thighs.

She stared down at it and smiled. She loved it, but she hadn't worn anything like this in ages. She wouldn't dare leave the house so exposed and...pretty. Could she wear it for Kestrel? Could she wear it in the privacy of her new extended family? If she got in that elevator and rode only to the basement and back up to the fifth floor, very few people would see her, and she trusted all of them.

"I bought it." He tapped her nose. "I bought you all kinds of clothes and had them delivered yesterday. Do you like it?"

She nodded, knowing she was smiling. "How did you know?"

He shrugged. "I guessed. I know you've been hiding under baggy clothes, ballcaps, and loose hair for a long time. You don't have to do that with me. You don't have to do that with Celeste or Sadie, or any of the guys. I couldn't be certain this is exactly the style you might prefer in the long run, but try it. Find yourself. Figure out who Zara is if she doesn't have to hide."

She smiled broader and then threw her arms around her

Daddy. "Thank you." She felt kind of choked up when she released him.

He pointed at the chair. "Sit. Let me dry your hair before we go downstairs."

"I can do it, Daddy." She reached for the comb he'd picked up again.

"Nope. Daddy will get you ready for the day as often as I can because I like taking care of you."

She sat and closed her eyes, going into her head while he turned on the hairdryer. Her world had changed drastically since her Daddy had walked into the laundry room and claimed her. She didn't even recognize herself. Who was this woman-slash-Little-girl, who wore a pink dress and spent the night naked, lying in a man's arms?

"Pigtails or braids?" Kestrel asked when he turned off the hairdryer.

She opened her eyes and stared at herself in the mirror. "Pigtails?" She had no idea. Like the dress, she would try one style and see how she felt.

Her Daddy deftly parted her hair down the middle, gathered one side, and secured a low pigtail right behind her ear. After he did the same on the other side, he added soft pink ribbons that matched her dress, tying them in pretty bows and then leaving the long tails hanging down her pigtails.

"How'd I do, Little Swan?"

Tears came to her eyes. "It's perfect, Daddy," she murmured.

He leaned over her and kissed her forehead. "There's a pair of matching ballet slippers next to the bed. How about if you brush your teeth and grab them so we can get downstairs?"

She quickly rose and grabbed her toothbrush, knowing he was probably pushing the clock a bit. Hurrying to join him, she grabbed the flats, slipped them on, and took just a moment to stare down at herself. The shoes fit perfectly, of course. Everything in her world was perfect lately.

Now, she had to hope this wasn't the calm before the storm.

Chapter Seventeen

"Storms are moving in." Those were the first words out of Magnus's mouth as Zara stepped out of the elevator with her Daddy. When Magnus spun around to face them, he abruptly stopped, his lips parted as though he were about to say more.

Zara flushed. He was staring at her.

"Magnus..." Kestrel warned.

Magnus jerked his attention to Kestrel and swallowed. "Sorry. I just wasn't expecting..."

The old fear that had always consumed Zara crept back into her as she wrapped her arm around her Daddy's and took a step behind him to hide. Maybe the dress hadn't been such a good idea. She could feel the tension coming from Kestrel.

Magnus spoke again. "I'm truly sorry, Zara. You just surprised me, is all. I've only seen you in jeans, baggy shirts, ball caps and sneakers. You look very pretty. I won't say another word."

She tipped her head back to look at her Daddy's expression. He was scowling at Magnus, but his face softened a bit as the seconds passed. Finally, he looked down at her. "He's right, Little Swan. Everyone might be surprised when they first see you because they aren't used to this style. I promise you can trust my teammates to treat you with respect."

She wasn't sure if her Daddy was saying that for her ears or as a warning to Magnus. Either way, she decided to be brave. She rose on her tiptoes, kissed her Daddy's cheek, and turned to skip toward the lab in search of Celeste.

She didn't look back, not wanting to know if one or both men were watching her. But she could hear them speaking in low voices not meant for her ears, and she could imagine her Daddy was chastising Magnus. She felt sorry for the computer guru. It really hadn't been his fault. She had to expect people to do a double take today, taking them off guard like this.

In fact, Celeste had nearly the same reaction when she turned around to face Zara. "Oh. Wow." Her eyes went wide. "That dress is so pretty."

Zara blew out a long breath. Celeste couldn't have said anything more perfect. *And again, with the "perfects."* "Thank you. Daddy bought it for me." Zara glanced down again and admitted, "It's been a long time since I've dressed in anything so revealing. I'm kind of nervous."

"No need. Sadie and I wear a lot of dresses when we're Little. Both our Daddies like to dress us, too." She had on a lab coat, but she unbuttoned the front of it to reveal a pretty yellow dress that was even more revealing and shorter than Zara's pink one.

Zara smiled. "I love your dress, too." She breathed out a sigh of relief. If Celeste and Sadie wore cute clothes, Zara wouldn't feel like she stood out. She reminded herself not to panic every time each member of the team saw her today.

Four more men and Sadie were going to go wide-eyed with shock. It was okay. They weren't ogling her or planning to kidnap her and sell her into sex trafficking. They were simply going to be surprised. That was all.

"Here." Celeste held out a lab coat. "Put this on. It'll give you some protection so you can ease into your new style."

"Do you think it suits me?" she asked as she took the coat, still looking down at herself. "I mean, it's so girly and so pink. I haven't worn anything girly or pink since I was a small child." *Except for my lingerie.*

Celeste took a seat in her swivel chair and pulled out a second one for Zara. "You've been hiding from the world for so long you probably don't even know who you are."

"Yes. That's it exactly." Zara smoothed her hand under her skirt as she sat.

Celeste shrugged. "All you can do is try different things and figure out what makes you comfortable. But that dress looks amazing on you. The pink complements your skin tone."

A noise at the doorway had them both swiveling to find Sadie stepping into the room. She was all professional, wearing black pants, a blouse, and low pumps. She also had a clipboard in her hand and a pencil tucked above her ear.

When she lifted her gaze, she stopped dead, mouth hanging open.

Zara couldn't help but giggle. She jumped up and spun around in a circle, causing her dress to flare out around her. "What do you think?"

"Oh my God. I love that dress!" Sadie stepped farther into the room.

"Right?" Celeste said, nodding.

Zara stopped spinning to face her new friends. Or maybe they were more like sisters. *Family.* She already felt closer to them than any other women she'd met. Even in college, she hadn't grown this close to other women.

Zara had always felt like she didn't quite fit in. Now, she wondered if perhaps the reason had been that she was Little and hadn't met anyone else with those same feelings.

Sadie looked down at her outfit. "I feel very boring now. After work, I'll tell Daddy to let me wear something pretty to dinner. Then we'll all be pretty."

Zara rolled her eyes. "You're always pretty, Sadie. You don't have to dress up to know that." She chewed on her bottom lip as she realized those words applied to her, too.

Celeste's calm voice came through again. "Before I came here, I was a lot like you, Zara. I rarely got dressed up. I didn't know anything about makeup. I spent every waking hour in a lab devoted to science. In the last several years, I had only dressed up one time for a gala. Several photos are still floating around social media of me in that dress. Every time I see it now, I smile. I felt good about myself that night. What matters is that we, as women, find our style and do what makes us feel good. Sometimes, that means honoring our true selves only in private spaces like this basement, but that's okay as long as we let our inner Littles out enough to feel happy."

Zara nodded slowly. "That was so lovely, Celeste. Thank you."

Sadie dabbed at a tear in the corner of her eye. "Yes," she whispered.

For a moment, the three of them stood there smiling at each other. For Zara, it felt life-affirming. Maybe she'd finally found her people. Could she really be a part of this family and stay here forever?

Sadie finally shook herself, straightened, and took a breath. "I almost forgot why I was down here." She tapped her clipboard. "I just printed out the weather report. There's a big storm coming in. We have top-notch generators and backup batteries, but make sure all your data is backed up. You never know what might happen in a power outage."

Celeste nodded. "Got it. Thank you."

Sadie spun around, but at the doorway, she looked over her shoulder. "I'm looking forward to a dress-up party tonight."

Zara stood to put on her lab coat and prepare to get to work, but before she had an arm in the sleeve, another body filled the doorway.

"Hey, girls..."

Zara lifted her gaze to find Phoenix leaning in, and she wasn't surprised to see that he, too, had stopped talking and stared at her, mouth open. He recovered faster, though. "Nice dress, Zara. I just came to tell you that we've canceled all the afternoon events. It won't be safe for rock climbing, scuba diving, or helicopter tours."

"Thanks for letting us know," Celeste said.

He nodded. "Hawking is beefing up security in case of a power outage, and he said to tell you he won't be able to join you for lunch, but, and I quote, if you don't order both breakfast and lunch and take the time to eat every bite, you can expect..." He smirked.

Zara held her breath, wondering what the other half of his sentence would be.

Celeste rolled her eyes. "Spit it out, Phoenix."

"I'm warning you. It's cheesy. I almost can't say it with a straight face, but I'm certainly going to catalog it in my head in case I ever meet the perfect Little girl for me."

"Phoenix..." Celeste groaned. "What?"

"Palm without balm." He roared with laughter as he turned and walked away.

Zara shifted her gaze to Celeste in confusion. "What does that mean?"

Celeste shook her head slowly. "He means he intends to spank my bottom hard and stand me in timeout without putting any soothing ointment on my naughty skin."

Zara gasped, eyes going wide. "Does he do that?"

"Hell, yes." Celeste slapped a hand over her mouth. "Don't tell Daddy I cussed. That will make it worse."

"But... But why?"

Celeste's eyes twinkled as she grinned. "Because I like it."

Zara continued to stare at Celeste's back after her friend turned away to check on the computer equipment. As Zara put her lab coat on, she told herself the reason she was so unnerved had nothing to do with the fact that her nipples were hard and her panties were wet—because that made no sense.

Chapter Eighteen

When the storm rolled in, it was so loud that Zara could hear the thunder booming even in the basement. She and Celeste had dutifully ordered breakfast and eaten every bite, but by the time lunch arrived, the two of them were scrambling to shut things down, just in case.

She knew where all the men were because they'd been given updates several times. Rocco was on the first floor at reception with Sadie, keeping a sharp eye on every guest coming and going since all six men were convinced there were nefarious guests at the resort.

Hawking was away from the main building at one of the security posts, helping his staff in case the cameras went out. He wanted as many eyes on every entrance and exit as possible.

Kestrel was out at the helipad, securing the helicopter. Obviously, this was the man Zara was most concerned about. She wished he was back here with her in the basement. But she kept reminding herself he had a job to do, and she needed to be a big girl and not complain.

She was safe here. After all, Magnus was frantically keeping an eye on every monitor in front of him, and Phoenix and Ceasar were also in the basement.

When Zara came out of the lab, she found herself fidgeting in the middle of the room. Several closets she hadn't seen before were open, and it looked like Phoenix and Caesar were doing some sort of inventory check. The closets were filled with ammunition and survival gear.

The sight of all that stuff made her hair stand on end. These men really were prepared for anything. The vibe in the basement was tense and unnerving.

She figured either Magnus or Kestrel had warned the rest of the men not to react to her dress because, after the shock she'd seen on Phoenix's face, no one else had said a word. They'd pretended she looked the same as any other day.

Zara felt antsy. There was a humming in the air. Was it the storm coming in or something more? Why was everyone scurrying around as though they were preparing for war?

When she looked down at her dress, she suddenly felt like she needed more clothes on. She also needed to get away from this madness around her for a few minutes.

She glanced toward the elevator and then back at Celeste as she joined her. "I'm going to go up and change," she told her friend.

"Oh, okay. Sure. Good idea. I might do that, too. This is a good afternoon for hot cocoa and snuggling in front of cartoons. Yoga pants. T-shirts." Celeste grinned. "Let's do it."

"Celeste." The booming voice came from Magnus, who held a phone up in the air over his shoulder without looking in their direction. "Hawking wants to talk to you."

Celeste sighed. "You go on ahead. I'll catch up with you in a minute."

While Celeste rushed toward Magnus, Zara scurried toward the elevator.

Caesar glanced in her direction as the doors slid open. "Where are you going, Little one?"

"Just to change."

"Okay. Fifth floor only. Come right back down," he ordered.

"I will." As the doors slid shut, she muttered, "So bossy. All of them." She lifted her thumb to activate the elevator so it would go straight to the fifth floor and waited.

It took a moment, but finally, the elevator moved. She watched the floors light up as it rose. *One more floor.* A fraction of a second after her thought, it lurched to a stop. She gripped the railing that encircled the walls of the structure, suddenly nervous. The lights flickered and went out a moment later.

Zara screamed on instinct as her heart started racing. In moments, emergency lights came on. They were dimmer, but at least she wasn't standing in the dark. "Shit," she murmured. The power must have gone out. Why did it have to happen while she was in the elevator?

She paced for a second. People knew she was in here. For certain, Celeste and Caesar were aware.

The clock ticked as she paced the small space. She wasn't ordinarily claustrophobic, but she didn't like being stuck in this elevator. Maybe all the sensors were down, and they didn't know she was trapped here.

When the elevator still hadn't moved a few minutes later, she decided she needed to help herself. "Hello?" she shouted. "Can anyone hear me?"

Nothing. More time passed. Seconds. Minutes. Probably not as much time as she thought.

"Hello?" she shouted louder.

"Zara? Is that you?"

Finally. She didn't recognize the voice, but relief made her blow out a long breath. "Yes."

"I'm with maintenance. They told me you were trapped in the elevator. We didn't know which floor you were on. I'm going to get the doors open. Just hang tight."

Thank God. She scooted back toward the wall, not wanting to be too close to the doors when they finally opened. She could hear people talking to each other, but she couldn't distinguish what they were saying.

"Hang tight, Zara. We're working on it," the man shouted.

"Okay." He probably couldn't hear her, but it didn't matter. She wanted out of this box.

Patience, Zara. They're working on it.

She sucked in a breath and held it when it sounded like the men were arguing. Suddenly, she felt unsure. Unease crept up her spine. She inched closer to the doors and put her ear against them.

"No, I don't have a fucking crowbar. I didn't know we were going to need it, asshole," one man muttered. Surely, the maintenance staff wouldn't speak to each other like that.

"Hello? Excuse me," Zara called out.

"We're working on it, Zara. Hang tight."

She didn't want them working on it anymore. "How did you know I was in here? Did Mr. Williams send you?"

"Uh, yes. Mr. Williams called us."

Shit. Zara backed up to the far wall. *Shit shit shit.* There was no Mr. Williams working for the hotel. At least not that she knew of.

"Don't worry, Zara. We're going to get you out of there."

Zara was shaking like a leaf now. She did not want these men to get to her. *Why didn't I bring my phone with me?* She could picture it on her desk in the lab. There was nothing she could do except scream bloody murder the moment they got these doors open.

Shit. Kestrel was going to be so mad. Not just at the situation but the fact that she'd gone upstairs alone. He hadn't explicitly told her to stay in the basement, and she'd taken the secure elevator. She would have stepped out on the fifth floor and gone into the secure apartment.

Now, these guys were going to get her.

A noise above her made her jerk her gaze up to the roof of the elevator. Her heart beat even faster, feeling like it would burst from her chest. Were they coming in from above to kidnap her?

Chapter Nineteen

"Where's Zara?" Kestrel barked into the room at large as soon as he stepped into the basement from the emergency stairwell. He'd run down the steps to reach her as soon as the power had flickered out. The emergency lights made the confined space with no windows look eerie—full of shadows and dark corners.

Phoenix turned from the open closet and looked around. "She was just here."

Magnus rose from his seat and glanced around, too.

Celeste was on the phone, ignoring them.

Caesar emerged from the bathroom. "What's wrong?" he asked as the three men looked in his direction.

"Have you seen Zara?" Kestrel nearly shouted.

"Yes. She went upstairs to change. She didn't make it back?"

"How long ago? Fuck! How long ago?" The hairs on Kestrel's neck stood on end.

"Not long. Maybe five or ten minutes. She must be on the

fifth floor and can't get back down. I'm sure she'll be right back down."

Kestrel turned toward the elevator and smashed his fist against the metallic doors. "The elevator is stuck somewhere. We couldn't turn on the auxiliary power. I'll go check the fifth floor. Try to call her," he yelled.

Without waiting for anyone to respond, he rushed back into the stairs. Where was she? Had she made it to the fifth floor, and now she was stuck up there? God, he hoped so. He hoped she hadn't decided to take the stairs. The stairwell wasn't secure. Only the elevator was secure.

"I'll go with you," Phoenix called out, pounding up the stairs behind Kestrel.

The two men powered up all five flights in record time, taking the steps three at a time. "Zara?" Kestrel shouted as he emerged into the joint living space. He ran to their apartment and yanked open the door. "Zara?"

Nothing. No response. He looked around. There was no evidence she'd been there. "Fuck." That meant she was stuck in the elevator.

"She's not up here," Phoenix added unnecessarily.

Magnus's voice came into Kestrel's com. "We have a problem, Kestrel."

"What?" he retorted.

"Three maintenance workers are on the fourth floor trying to get the elevator to open."

"Good." *How was that a problem?* "Zara's in there."

"Not good at all, man. I've never seen those guys. They don't work for us."

All the blood ran from Kestrel's face as he ran back out of the apartment and headed for the elevator. "Do you have eyes on them?"

He glanced at Phoenix. Phoenix was listening to the same conversation through his own comm unit.

"Yes. They're still working to open the doors. They don't have any equipment."

Stay calm. She's fine. "And you think the elevator is stuck on the fourth floor?"

"Affirmative."

Kestrel rushed to the elevator doors. "Can you get these open for me?"

"I can," Phoenix stated as he stepped up to a panel. He opened it, tapped several buttons, and then set his thumb on a pad.

Suddenly, the doors opened. Thank fuck.

Kestrel leaned over the open shaft to find the top of the elevator only a few feet below him.

"Make sure this elevator doesn't start back up," Phoenix commanded into the comm unit.

"On it," Magnus stated. "I've disabled it. Can you get to her?"

"Yes. What's the status of the men on the fourth floor?" Phoenix asked.

"They're still working on it. One of them left. He just returned with a crowbar. Where the hell did he find a crowbar?" Magnus growled.

Kestrel was listening to them, but he had already jumped down on top of the elevator. The moment he landed, he heard Zara squeal. Without a word, he opened the escape hatch on the top, dropped onto his stomach, and leaned his head into the elevator.

She must have heard him land on the roof. She had her head tipped back and was squished into the corner of the elevator. When she saw him, her eyes widened.

"Take my hand, Little Swan," he said as softly and calmly as possible.

A noise coming from the doors made her jerk her gaze in that direction.

Kestrel's blood pressure shot through the roof. "Zara, Little girl, now. Take my hand." He scooted his body closer and leaned in as far as he dared.

She was frozen with fear. He could read the signs. He could also hear the men on the other side of those doors grumbling. The sound of metal scraping against metal scared the fuck out of him.

"Zara," he said louder. "I'm going to spank your butt so red if you don't grab my hand. Now, Little girl."

That seemed to reach her. She nodded before finally jerking herself to her feet to take two strides to get to him, reaching up with her hand at the same time.

The moment he could grab her, Kestrel wrapped his hand around her wrist and pulled. Thank God she weighed so little and didn't fight him. He pulled her slim body up through the escape hatch, stood her on her feet next to him, and was just dropping the door back into place when the elevator doors slid open.

"Where is she?" one of the men yelled as he tipped his head back to look up.

Kestrel made eye contact with him. The fucker was lucky Kestrel's only goal was to get his Little girl to safety. If she hadn't been standing next to him in this elevator shaft, scared out of her mind, Kestrel would have jumped down into the elevator and taken all three of those men out with his bare hands. There was no telling what he might have done to them.

What made his blood boil strongest was the fact that he recognized that man. He was the same man who had gone on two helicopter excursions this week—the one who had aroused his suspicions.

Kestrel dropped the door back into place and stood on it. He needed to buy a few seconds. Turning to lift Zara by the waist, he delivered her into Phoenix's strong hands, and the big man pulled her up in a massive display of strength and urgency.

"Please tell me someone is on their way to grab those assholes," Kestrel shouted into the comm as he scrambled hand over hand up the elevator cable to haul himself out of the shaft. Without pausing, he grabbed Zara around the waist, lifted her into his arms, and rushed her into the fifth-floor living space as Phoenix worked his magic on the elevator doors.

Kestrel heard them slam shut and relaxed slightly. To his relief, Phoenix had already opened the door into their living area, leaving it for them to dash inside. Kestrel slammed it closed and secured it as soon as they were all inside. The fifth floor wasn't a safe room like the basement, but it would take someone with a lot of gunpower or explosives to get through the door.

"They got away," Magnus stated a moment later. "Caesar went up the stairs as fast as he could, but they're gone. Rocco and Hawking are coming this direction. We've got eyes every-where. We'll try to intercept them before they get too far."

Kestrel dropped onto the couch, still holding Zara in his arms. He cradled her in his lap and held her tightly, burying his face in her hair. He'd almost lost her.

She started sobbing. Her entire body shook. "I'm so sorry, Daddy. I shouldn't have come upstairs alone. I'm so, so sorry."

He rocked her gently, inhaling her scent, trying to control his breathing. When he finally gave her enough space to breathe and lean back, she met his gaze. Her lip was trembling, and tears were running down her face. "Are you mad at me?"

He brushed a stray lock of hair from her face. "No, Little Swan. I'm not mad. I'm just so glad we got to you. I was scared." Scared was an understatement. Kestrel had been fucking terrified out of his mind, but he didn't want to send her into a panic.

They all jumped when the door opened. Caesar walked in, shut it, and resecured it. "Lost them." He was breathing heavily.

"I'm so sorry," Magnus said into the comm. He sounded furious. "I have so many monitors running, and I've been switching around among them, trying to keep eyes on as many camera angles as I can, all at the same time. I didn't know Zara went upstairs. I wasn't watching the elevator on every floor."

"It's not your fault," Kestrel responded as calmly as possible. He was stroking his Little girl all up and down her back, her face, her legs. Touching her everywhere to reassure himself she was here in his arms. She was fine. Unharmed.

This time.

Chapter Twenty

"Is she sleeping?"

Kestrel turned toward Sadie as he stepped into the living room and quietly shut the door to his apartment. With full power restored, the common space was illuminated brightly, dispelling all the shadows. "Yeah."

Celeste was with Sadie. The two women were huddled on the couch, holding each other. Hawking and Rocco were standing behind them. The two Daddies had rushed to be with their Littles as fast as they could.

Kestrel couldn't blame them. It would be a while before any of them let their Little girls out of their sight again.

Except Zara was not in Kestrel's line of sight right now. She'd been exhausted, and he'd tucked her into the daybed in the playroom, where she'd fallen fast asleep. It had taken him time to be able to leave her, even knowing she was the safest there. Eventually, the need to reassure the other Littles and strategize with his teammates had convinced him to leave her playroom.

Kestrel glanced back at the door to the apartment he

shared with Zara, noting the pretty swan picture they'd hung up. Had that been just yesterday? It seemed like they'd lived a lifetime since she'd colored that picture.

Both Sadie and Celeste had red, swollen eyes from crying.

"Is she okay?" Celeste asked.

"She will be." Kestrel sat in one of the armchairs and looked toward Rocco and then Hawking. "This can't be her life. Always hiding and on the run." He was concerned. He prayed to God all of these people trying to kidnap her were working for the same man. If he could somehow manage to take down this particular operation, would another human trafficking ring pick up where these guys left off?

Yes, she was pretty. There were a lot of pretty people in the world. Granted, not all of them had been featured in several magazines, drawing attention to them. There was no way to undo the past, though. All they could do was find a way to create a path forward, one in which Zara could live in peace without constantly worrying that someone would kidnap her.

Zara had said her father was old friends with Kingsley. It was past time to give Kingsley a call and ask a few dozen questions. It was also time to make contact with Zara's parents, especially her father. The man needed to know that his daughter was not only under Kestrel's protection but that she would be for the rest of her life. There wasn't a chance in hell Kestrel would let Zara go back home when this finally over.

He knew deep in his heart she was his, and he was confident she knew it, too. Her new life was here with him, with her new extended family. He hoped it would help his case that she seemed to love working with Celeste. That part was certainly convenient.

A fierce sense of overprotectiveness consumed Kestrel. He hated that the three men had not only gotten away, but they'd already managed to leave the resort. The storm had hindered Magnus and the rest of the men. The computer expert hadn't been able to watch every single camera. Along with the observations of the team who'd searched the property after the incident, Magnus had been able to piece together just enough data to confirm that the men had snuck off the property and disappeared.

The door to the living room opened, and Magnus and Caesar stepped inside.

Magnus had his ballcap drawn lower over his eyes than usual. He dropped onto the corner of the couch and ran a hand down his face. "I pulled all the footage I could find from before the electricity went out. Based on the looks on those guys' faces, I'm going to bet they got lucky when they heard someone calling for help from the elevator. Granted, I suspect they were snooping around that shaft because they suspected we were harboring Zara somewhere that was only accessible by that one elevator, but the looks on their faces when they realized she was stuck in that elevator speak volumes. They were nearly giddy with delight. And they were equally fucking pissed when you pulled her to safety. I've also never seen three people run so fast. They knew we were going to be on them in seconds."

"We should have gotten them," Kestrel growled.

"We should have. I'm sorry. I should've checked that she'd arrived. It's on me," Caesar said, running his hand over his face as if trying to erase the stressed expression that was carved into it.

"It wasn't your fault, Caesar. It was a perfect storm." A huge crash of thunder interrupted Kestrel as if adding an exclamation point to his words.

"We were divided all over the resort, preparing for the storm. Hawking got the backup generators on to provide emergency lighting. No one could watch everything," Kestrel said, erasing the blame from his teammate.

Nods followed around the room. Kestrel knew that no one would allow a single member of the team to shoulder all the responsibility. There were elements totally out of their control. He ran his fingers through his hair in frustration.

"I'm going in there to hold my Little girl. I think we need to monitor the cameras tonight to make sure they don't come back," Kestrel suggested. Phoenix was down there now, keeping an eye on everything and listening in by comm so Magnus could come up and share his findings directly.

"I've got it," Magnus assured him.

"You can't do it all," Caesar corrected him. "I'll take the next four hours after Phoenix while you grab some sleep."

Magnus bristled and opened his mouth to argue before pausing and nodding. "Thanks. I'm running on empty."

"I'll relieve you for the next shift," Hawking chimed in.

"I don't need to sleep that long," Magnus said, shaking his head.

"If you wake up, you can join them. They can watch the real-time feeds while you look for clues from old footage, Magnus," Sadie suggested.

"Good idea," Magnus reluctantly agreed.

"We also have to figure out a long-term plan to keep Zara safe," Kestrel said, thrusting his fingers through his hair in exasperation. "She needs to be able to live her life and not hide from the bad guys in the world."

"Go stay with her, Kestrel. We'll all try to come up with something," Hawking suggested.

Nodding, Kestrel headed back to his rooms. He patted

the swan as he reached the door. Little Swan. He had to keep her safe.

Walking through the darkened room, he saw her curled into a ball in the narrow playroom bed. Kestrel stripped off his clothes and climbed behind her, wrapping himself around her curved form. Without a pause in her breathing, Zara shifted back a fraction of an inch to plaster herself against him. Kestrel pressed a kiss to her shoulder.

"Daddy," she whispered. Her breath sighed out as he felt her relax against him.

"I'm here, Little Swan."

Kestrel forced himself to sleep with her. His military training had taught him to take advantage of opportunities to recharge. Rousing each time she shifted or bumped him with an elbow, he soothed her with a kiss on her shoulder or neck.

"Noooo!"

Kestrel's eyelids flew open. His hands smoothed over her shoulder to calm Zara, but she scooted away, holding her arms out to keep him away.

"I don't want to go! Stop! You can't make me!"

"Zara, it's okay. I'm not going to let them take you. You're safe here, Little girl," Kestrel rushed to reassure her.

"They're after me! They won't stop until they get me," she sobbed as she flailed her arms around to ward him off.

"Wake up all the way, Zara." Kestrel spoke to her sternly, trying to break through the terror that filled her mind.

She shook her head frantically, and Kestrel knew she was trapped in a nightmare she couldn't escape. Mentally flying through options, he chose one. Ignoring her strikes to his body, Kestrel captured her lips and kissed her with every ounce of love in his heart. Her body froze for several long seconds as he showed her how much he cared for her. When she softened against him and encircled his neck with her arms, he knew he'd reached her.

Feathering light kisses on her lips, Kestrel stroked up and down her spine. When she wiggled closer and thrust her fingers through his hair to pull his lips solidly against hers, he again deepened his kiss. Zara responded instantaneously.

His hands swept under the T-shirt he'd draped around her body before tucking her in bed. "Arms up, Little Swan," he ordered firmly before whisking it over her head as she complied.

Immediately, she wiggled back next to him as if needing the skin-to-skin contact. Kestrel wrapped an arm around her to hold her close. He pressed soft kisses to her neck and shoulders, aiming only to soothe her.

"Hard, Daddy. Make my thoughts stop," she begged.

Hating the tremor in her voice, Kestrel dedicated himself to wiping away what must have been an endless loop of reliving her experience. He kissed her hard, forcing a response as he explored the depth of her mouth. Her tongue tangled with his as she threw herself into their exchange.

Kestrel brushed a hand over her shoulder and then up her torso, cradling one full breast in his hand. He squeezed, and she gasped into his mouth. Immediately, he bent to pull her beaded nipple into his mouth with firm suction. Her fingers tangled in his hair, pulling slightly, returning the hint of pain—not tugging him away but helping to distract him as well. He rolled her nipple between his teeth, biting her just enough to make her moan in pleasure as his fingers traced patterns on the sensitive underswell of her breast.

While repeating his attentions to her other side, Kestrel drew his fingertips lightly down the center of her body. He loved the feel of her body quivering under his touch as he neared the slightly rounded mound. Stopping just above her cleft, Kestrel raised his mouth from her body.

Her eyes flew open as his caresses stopped. With their gazes meshed, Kestrel promised her, "You are mine, Little girl. I will always protect what belongs to me."

"Yes, Daddy," she whispered.

"Now, I'm going to fuck you so hard you can't think of anything else."

His coarse words made her eyes widen. Slowly, she nodded, "Please, Daddy."

Kestrel rolled their entwined bodies over to balance her on top of him. "Sit up, Little Swan."

He helped her move into position. "Straddle my face, Zara," he directed firmly.

She looked at him in shock, and he almost read her thoughts. "Straddle you?" she echoed.

"The best view in the world." His hands cupped her slim thighs, and he lifted her into position. Holding her elevated above him, Kestrel savored her display. "So beautiful. But I need to taste you. Sit, Little girl."

"I can't do that," she whispered furiously.

"Refusing to do what your Daddy says? That's twenty spanks. Want to earn more?"

Instantly, she shook her head.

"Good girl." He drew her down to his mouth and held her in place. Nibbling at the buffet she presented, Kestrel enjoyed her sweet taste as he searched for the most responsive spots.

Her thighs trembled as she tried to hold herself slightly above him, and Kestrel tugged her lower to rest on his lips. He could tell immediately when Zara stopped worrying about smothering him and focused on the sensations he lavished on her body. Her squirms and gasps delighted him as she lost herself in pleasure. When her quivers strengthened around his tongue as he explored her, Kestrel lifted her away.

"Wait!" she cried.

"Not yet, Little girl. Daddy's not done playing."

Wrapping his hands around her waist, he shifted her across his hips. Kestrel drew her back against his body so her wetness pressed over his rigid cock. "Make yourself come."

Her gaze met his. Bravely, she shifted forward on top of his shaft and gasped. Her movements quickened as he caressed her body. Kestrel treasured the view of her breasts swaying above him as she concentrated on pushing the sensations inside her higher and higher. Reaching up, he cupped her gorgeous tits and tweaked her taut peaks.

"Ahhh!"

That taste of sweet pain pushed her into a climax that rocked her body over him. Without allowing her to recover, Kestrel rose to wrap his arms around her. He kissed her hard, letting her taste herself on his lips. Her tongue swiped over his skin, savoring her own flavor. Need exploded inside him at this erotic sight.

Kestrel had to feel her wrapped around him. With a growl, he lifted her hips to fit his cock to her drenched opening. As her tremors continued, he drew her body down to his. He loved how her eyes widened as he filled the space inside her.

"So good," she whispered.

"Just wait, Little Swan," he promised.

His fingers bit into the soft flesh of her hips as he lifted and lowered her body over his. With each downstroke, he ground his pelvis against hers. Her fingernails bit into his shoulders as she clung to him. He treasured every kiss, every gasp, every shiver.

Their skin dampened as the heat built in the playroom.

Her scent pushed his arousal higher. Kestrel could feel her body tightening around him. The shimmers heralding her climax threatened to push him over the edge.

"Eyes on me, Little girl," he ordered, holding her gaze with his. Looking into those gorgeous blue eyes, he growled, "Come now, Zara."

"Yes!" she screamed into the room, never looking away as her body clamped around him.

The intimacy of the moment etched itself into Kestrel's heart as he relaxed his iron-clad control to empty himself into her. Cupping the back of her head, he kissed her hard, staking his claim for all time.

She slumped against him, allowing Kestrel to support her. He held her tightly, pressing kisses to her face and shoulders as their bodies calmed. When she nestled—her breath settling into a regular pattern—he lowered them back to the mattress. Still deep inside her, Kestrel held Zara close on the narrow bed as she drifted back to sleep—this time, rested and nourished.

Chapter Twenty-One

Heat surrounded her. Zara snuggled a bit closer to the warming source as she blinked her eyes open. A brown stubble appeared. Tilting her head back a touch, she saw Kestrel's chiseled jaw and his beautiful lips. Zara licked hers, remembering just how talented he was with his mouth. She'd actually sat on his face!

Nothing was taboo with her Daddy. He loved her completely, and he intended to love all of her completely. That was super arousing and challenging. His dominance drew her like a moth to a flame. It felt dangerous.

And I like it.

Her lips curved into a smile at that thought. Zara dawdled lazily in bed, hoping Kestrel wouldn't wake up. She didn't want to disturb him, and cuddling next to his powerful body was definitely not a burden.

Her bladder wouldn't tolerate her laziness long. Fearful of losing control, Zara eased herself away from him and fled to the bathroom, pausing briefly to close the bedroom door. In a flash, she accomplished her mission and washed her face and hands. Not wanting to wake her Daddy, she grabbed a washcloth and cleaned up at the sink.

Kestrel had made space for her big-girl clothes in his closet and had even given her drawer space to unpack. After pulling a drawer open, she grabbed a pair of panties and a bra. Donning them quickly, she found a pair of jeans and a T-shirt in his closet.

Dressed, she hesitated.

What should she do now? Stay in their apartment? Go into the common area to avoid waking Kestrel up? She really wanted to go downstairs and immerse herself in the research Celeste was conducting. Doing that by herself didn't seem smart.

"You're very overdressed, Little girl," a sleepy voice observed from the doorway into the playroom.

"Daddy! I didn't want to wake you up." She studied his form, dressed only in low-riding jeans. His chiseled body looked scrumptious, and Zara had a flashback to their love-making last night.

"I like whatever thought just flitted through your mind. Next time, wake me up, Little Swan. I would've worried about you if I'd found you missing when I woke up."

"I was going to leave a note," she suggested.

"Next time, wake me up," he responded sternly.

"Yes, Daddy," she answered.

"Good girl. Come give me a kiss."

Zara flew across the room to him and wrapped her arms around his waist. Closing her eyes, she puckered her lips and waited. When seconds passed by with no touch of his mouth on hers, she peeked with one eye.

"Give me a kiss, Little girl," he repeated.

"Oh!" Feeling her face heat with embarrassment that she had misunderstood, Zara rose onto her tiptoes to press her lips to his. She put all her emotions into her kiss, wanting him to know how deeply she felt for him. He tugged her closer as he responded to her. By the time she dropped down from her toes, they were both breathing heavily.

"Thank you for the kiss, Zara. That's the way I always want to start my day. Now, I have to shower before work, but would you like to go downstairs to the lab?"

"Yes, please."

"Do you need to clean up?" he asked.

This time, her heated face was an inferno. Her gaze dropped to the floor, and she admitted, "I already took a sponge bath."

He lifted her chin until he could look into her eyes. "It's okay to be messy at times. Daddy's the one who got you that way," he reminded her.

"Daddy!" she protested, squirming in front of him.

"And you know what?"

"What?"

"I plan to do it again and again."

"Promise?" she asked, feeling her embarrassment pushed away by the allure of his future lovemaking.

"I promise." His slow wink went straight to her heart. "I love you, Little girl."

"I love you, Daddy. Can I come shower with you?"

"Of course. We don't have time to play this morning, but I'll make it up to you."

"Yes, please, Daddy." She batted her eyelashes at him provocatively.

"You're going to kill me," he said before visibly forcing himself to step back. Offering his hand, Kestrel led her into the bathroom.

"That was so scary," Celeste said, shaking her head. "I think I would have been frozen with fear."

"Not if your Daddy was ordering you to take his hand," Zara pointed out.

"You're right. That and the bad guys were coming in the door. How fast was your heart pounding?" Sadie asked.

"Like it was going to jump out of my chest," Zara admitted.

"Are they gone?" Celeste asked.

"I don't know. Maybe?" Zara said before she felt her shoulders slump. "Probably not. They never seem to go away. I've even thought of having some kind of surgery. Maybe a scar would make them leave me alone."

"You don't even want to think about something like that. Our Daddies are going to protect you. Your Daddy won't let anything happen to you," Sadie assured her.

"I know, but I don't want anything to happen to him either," Zara said, her eyes filling with tears.

Instantly, Sadie and Celeste swarmed closer to hug her between them. Zara stood between the best friends she'd ever had and hugged them back fiercely. Thank goodness for whatever had brought her here.

An image of her parents flashed into her brain. She was so far away. Would she ever see them again?

"Zara?"

At the sound of Kestrel's voice, she blinked away the moisture from her eyes. "Yes, Daddy. The Littles were just comforting me."

"I'm glad your friends are supporting you. I'm sorry to

interrupt, but Magnus is working on something important for us. Come with me to the computer area."

"Really? Is he tracking down the bad guys?" Zara asked. She gave her friends one last squeeze before wiggling out of the middle of the hug fest.

"He is, but this isn't related to that," Kestrel shared. He wrapped his arm around her as Zara joined him and steered her out of the area by the lab.

As they approached Magnus's station, she heard his voice loud and clear. "Mr. Flores, please hold on. I promise you this is no hoax. Your daughter is here."

Zara ran at the sound of the Mexican accent that answered.

"Papá? Mamá?" she called as she skidded to a stop in front of one of Magnus's large display screens. Tears streamed down her face at the sight of her parents' concerned expressions. She interlaced her fingers with Kestrel's when he wrapped his arm around her waist. Leaning against his body, she relied on his support.

"*Mija!*" her mother greeted her. "Don't cry, my love. You will make us all cry. Are you unhappy?"

Dashing away her tears, Zara immediately shook her head and assured her, "No. I'm happy here."

"I'm glad, *mija*. Who is this man next to you? And are you safe there?" her father asked, his expression darkening.

"My name is Kestrel Galison, Mr. Flores. I am one of the team Mr. Kingsley entrusted with your daughter's safety." He tugged Zara closer and added, "I love Zara and will protect her with my life."

"You love my daughter?" Zara's mother repeated, looking shocked.

"I do."

"I love him, too, *Mamá*," Zara rushed to assure her parents.

"Zara..." her father said hesitantly. She could read his mind. He didn't think she'd been gone long enough to have true, strong emotions about this man.

"I assure you, sir, that our feelings are solid and long-term. I contacted you today on this secured line, so that you could talk to your daughter, and we could update you on her status here."

Zara nodded. "I'm working in a secure lab for Celeste Blanke. She's the research scientist who was on the news for making a huge breakthrough on how cancer will be treated," Zara told her parents.

"That's exciting, Zara, but are you safe?" her father refocused the conversation.

"We foiled an attack last night, Mr. Flores. Unfortunately, traffickers appear to have attempted to target her here as well. We guess that they must have seen her during Zara's trip to Danger Bluff."

"Baldwin assured me she would be safe there," Mr. Flores asserted.

"I am safe here, *Papá*. There was a storm that knocked out the electricity. Some bad guys took advantage of the situation. D—Kestrel saved me," Zara told him quickly. "All the guys worked together to keep me safe."

"Are you happy there, Zara? More protected there than here? Maybe we made a mistake. Maybe you should come home," her mother suggested, focusing on her daughter.

"I'm staying with Kestrel. He won't let anyone hurt me. None of the team will."

"You'll keep her from harm?" Mr. Flores asked, pinning Kestrel in place with a steely-eyed look.

"I will," Kestrel promised without hesitation.

At Magnus's signal, he added, "I'm afraid we can't protect the line any longer, Mr. and Mrs. Flores. We'll have to say goodbye."

"Call again! I love you," Mrs. Flores said quickly.

Magnus severed the connection. "It's good. No one was able to piggyback on the call. I'll stay alert, but I'm confident we're fine."

Zara turned and threw herself into Kestrel's arms. Tears rolled down her face once again. "Thank you, Magnus. I was so glad to see them."

"They needed to know that you had people watching over you. I needed them to know that I've claimed you," Kestrel told her as he stroked her back to reassure her.

Clinging to him, she nodded. She had loved seeing her parents. They meant the world to her, but she'd found who she was supposed to be in New Zealand. Kestrel was the man she'd always dreamed about and never imagined finding. Working with Celeste... Her friends... She treasured every moment that she had now. Who knew how long this could last?

"Kingsley here," the voice on the phone announced. "I was waiting to talk to you alone."

An eerie feeling went down his spine at the thought that Kingsley knew from a distance that he was not with others. Shrugging that off, Kestrel scanned the area. The billionaire who owned the resort could check into the cameras whenever he wanted. Kestrel was almost at the helicopter pad but far enough away that he could find a quiet space to talk.

"Kingsley, tell me what's going on," Kestrel prompted.

"Have I told you the helicopter footage of your last tour was amazing?" the older man asked with a rumble of humor.

"I think you're much too busy to bother telling me that."

"You're right. I know you have Magnus, who's one of the best at picking up chatter, but my sources caught news of a sale of one of the highest traffickers' targets."

"Zara?" Kestrel asked.

"The name is never used. It's possible. Highly probable, I should say."

"We've been on high alert since the first attempt. But thanks. I'll make sure someone is with Zara at all times."

"Thank you. She's special to me. I've known her family for years. Her father and I have...collaborated in the past. Zara was as precious as a child as she is today."

"You knew she would be my Little," Kestrel stated.

"I had a strong suspicion," Kingsley hedged. "Life can never be certain. I will forward Magnus any information I have and anything that comes up in the future."

Feeling the end of the conversation approaching, Kestrel said, "Kingsley, I never got to thank you for saving me. Repaying the marker has given me the one I never thought I'd find. You have my gratitude."

There was silence on the other end of the line for a few seconds, and Kestrel knew he had surprised the mastermind behind so many rescues. That felt like it should mean something.

"Take care of Zara, Kestrel."

"I will, sir."

A click signaled the end of the conversation, making Kestrel stare at the blank screen. A smile curved his lips. Knowing there were people in the world serving as a force for good in the vast quagmire of predatory forces gave him hope. Nodding, he walked back to the path and on to his next tour.

Chapter Twenty-Two

"We need to have a party," Celeste announced that afternoon in the lab.

"A party?" Zara echoed.

She was trying so hard not to look at the clock. Coming down the elevator had been traumatic this morning. Her Daddy had wrapped her in his arms and lifted her like a frozen statue to carry her inside when she hadn't been able to step into the metal box. Zara knew she'd have to do it again.

"Hey, are you okay?" Celeste asked.

"No. We have two hours left before dinner, and then I'll have to get back into the elevator." Zara tried to breathe, but her chest was tight.

"Should I call your Daddy?" Celeste asked, steering her out of the area where they were conducting experiments.

"No. I don't want to worry him. I'll be okay. I have to be okay. I just keep remembering the hatch being flung open, and then the metallic sounds of them prying open the doors," Zara said, shivering.

Celeste hugged her close. "I can't imagine. Just hearing

about it scares me. But your Daddy saved you. He's not going to let anything happen to you."

"He can't be everywhere."

"If your Daddy isn't there, then another of the team will step in. Do you think my Daddy would ever let anything happen to you?" Celeste asked.

"No," Zara admitted, shaking her head. "It's just so scary, knowing so many people are after me. You understand; I heard about your story on the news."

"Our guys seem to have a thing for women in trouble. I think we need to make them matching superhero capes," Celeste teased, making Zara chuckle as she visualized all the hunky guys in spandex with their capes blowing in the wind.

"Are you seeing what I'm seeing in my head?" Zara asked, pushing back a bit to look at her friend's face.

"I could love tight body suits." Celeste waggled her eyebrows suggestively.

"We are so bad." Zara snickered. To her relief, she felt the anxiety that had threatened to overwhelm her slide away for a bit.

"So bad, we deserve to party," Celeste said with a wink.

"Let's do it!"

"Yes. We can have it upstairs in the common area. We'll wear pretty dresses and do our hair. The guys can order party food for us. Maybe we'll even dance," Celeste suggested.

"Is there a particular reason for a party? Is it your birthday or Sadie's?"

"There doesn't have to be a reason, silly. We can have a party because it's Friday or Saturday—even a Monday!" Celeste assured her.

"I haven't been to a party in years."

"Then I think it's time."

Celeste picked up her phone and sent a text. A split second later, the phone buzzed in her hand. "Sadie's in."

"Now, we just need to convince the guys," Zara said.

"Convince us of what?" Kestrel's deep voice from the doorway made the two women whirl around.

"You scared me." With a nervous laugh, Zara put her hand on her thudding heart.

"Sorry. I had a short break and wanted to check on you. Are you okay?" he asked, moving forward to hug her.

"I'm okay," she whispered into the crook of his neck.

"Good." Kestrel stepped away and said, "Now. Tell me what's going on, Little girl."

"We want to have a party," Zara said. When his face looked skeptical, his eyebrows shooting upward, she added quickly, "Upstairs on the fifth floor, where it's safe. No one would know."

"A party, hmmm?"

"Please, Daddy. It will be fun," Zara said, trying to convince him.

"Let me talk to the team," he said, grimacing.

"And if they say yes?"

"Then, we'll have a small gathering with music and food," Kestrel relented.

"A party!" she said, knowing he would twist arms if he had to in order to please her.

Celeste rushed forward to hug Zara. The two Littles jumped up and down in a circle, celebrating. Sadie ran through the doorway at breakneck speed and joined the fun. Chants of *party, party, party* filled the air.

"What is going on here?" Magnus asked with a concerned look. "Sadie just ran through here as if her life depended on it."

"Know of any reason they can't have a party on the top floor?" Kestrel battled keeping the corners of his mouth from curling up at his usually unflappable teammate's expression.

"What are we celebrating?" Magnus asked.

"Life?" Kestrel responded.

"I'm going back to my computers. Everything makes more sense there." Magnus shook his head, pulled his cap lower on his forehead, and turned to stalk out of the room.

"All right, Little girls. Magnus is on board," he said, chuckling. "Who's going to talk to Caesar, Phoenix, Hawking, and Rocco?"

"I've got Daddy and Phoenix!" Celeste said excitedly, claiming two.

"I've got Daddy and Caesar!" Sadie volunteered. "Let's go now, Celeste."

"I'll be back in a few minutes, Zara," Celeste promised. "Watch the chemical reaction that's brewing and note the changes you see."

"On it." Zara returned to the experimental table of the science area.

Kestrel followed and heard a big sigh ease from his Little's lips. "Hey, what's the matter? Do you not want to have a party? I can be the bad guy and squelch the idea."

"Oh, no! I want to have fun with my friends. I haven't been to a party with friends since I was small. There was a problem with one of my friend's dads, and my parents wouldn't allow me to go to anyone's house again."

Controlling his pissed-off expression with a steel will, Kestrel said, "Another great reason to have a party. Do you need a new dress?"

"A new dress?" Zara blinked at him as she thought. "Oh, I can wear the pretty dress I wore before."

"A new dress, it is. What color?"

"Really? I mean, I'd love to wear the other dress. You don't have to get me anything," she said quickly.

"I know I don't have to. I want to. Do you want me to choose?"

"Yes, please." Zara nodded happily.

"I'll do that this afternoon. I'm off to give a tour, Little girl. Be good."

When Kestrel turned to leave, she asked, "Are you going to order anything else?"

"What do you need, Little Swan? I have a few things on my list to get for you."

"Would it be possible to get a few things for our apartment?"

"Sure. Another chair?"

"No. I think we need something colorful. Maybe some pillows? Something for the walls? Everything is so colorful and happy back in Mexico. In my parents' house, the walls are yellow, and the furniture is in all sorts of bright hues."

"Things are pretty dull in our space. I bet that seems sad to you. We'll choose some things together tonight. You think about a new color for the walls," he directed before stepping forward to press a kiss to her lips. "Never hesitate to ask for anything, Little girl. You can always talk to me."

"Thanks, Daddy."

"I'll see you this evening for dinner. Then we'll go do some shopping online."

He loved the sweet smile that spread over her lips. With one last peck, he hurried away to his next flight. Damn, he loved her.

Chapter Twenty-Three

Several days later, Zara was finally able to ignore the scratches on the sides of the elevator doors. Her Daddy still rode with her, but he didn't have to carry her inside. The team had brought in more powerful generators to make any lapse of electricity undetectable by guests. They would know when the auxiliary power took over, but it would be a faint hiccup to everyone else.

According to Sadie, the influx of single men coming to the resort had slacked off as well. Even Magnus seemed more at ease if that was possible. The team and Sadie had settled into their groove of supporting the Danger Bluff resort, and things ran like clockwork. Her time with Kestrel was limited by her work in the lab and his flight schedule, but her Daddy definitely helped her enjoy every minute together.

"You're thinking very hard, Little girl," Kestrel murmured as they sat at the dinner table.

"Sorry, Daddy. Just thinking back over everything that's happened. Do you think it's over?" The look on his face answered her, and she slumped against him.

"Hey, Kestrel. I put a ton of delivery boxes in your apartment this afternoon," Caesar called across the table. "Remind me never to walk past the registration desk."

"I wondered how I was going to get the mail delivered up there. Thank you for helping," Sadie said with a smile. Everyone knew Caesar would be the first to help in any situation.

"We have boxes?" Zara asked, sitting up, invigorated.

"Eat, Little girl. Then we'll go rip open cardboard. Did you all decide what time the party starts tomorrow?" Phoenix asked.

"We wanted to start at eight, but our Daddies were concerned it would go past our bedtimes. So, we're starting at seven," Celeste said with a meaningful look at Hawking.

"Be good, Little girl. I would hate for you not to be able to sit at the party," Hawking warned with his own message-laden glance.

"Seven o'clock is a great time. You guys are coming, aren't you?" Sadie asked, looking at Magnus, Caesar, and Phoenix.

"Not me. I'm manning the cameras," Magnus immediately said to excuse himself.

"You couldn't take one night off to dance?" Celeste asked.

"I don't dance."

"We could teach you," Zara suggested. "You know, so you can dance with...someone important in the future."

"I doubt if Baldwin Kingsley III will magically produce my Little girl," Magnus said in a skeptical tone.

"Who knows?" Zara countered. "He sent me and Sadie here. Celeste is a mystery. She thinks she remembers seeing an ad promising a getaway where you can escape from everyone. Maybe he had something to do with that appearing where she'd see it...?"

"I don't doubt that he could make that happen, but

finding a Little girl who's a match with me will be the challenge of a lifetime. I know. I haven't found her," Magnus pointed out.

Zara shrugged and nodded at Kestrel. "I'm pretty sure our Daddies searched to find us, too. Who knows—maybe Mr. Kingsley is a Little-Daddy whisperer?"

"Next time, I'll attend your party. Okay, Little girl?" Magnus said nicely to put her off.

"I'm going to hold you to that."

Shaking his head, Magnus took a bite and groaned as Hawking picked up the silver serving spoon in the center of the table.

"I have balloons for the party. I'm counting on everyone to help me blow them up. Magnus, I already put a bag on your keyboard," Hawking informed him with a smirk before continuing, "Sadie, did you get the desserts and snacks ordered for the party?"

Sadie nodded from her position, sitting on Rocco's lap. She was busy putting Band-Aids on her Daddy's fingers from his rock-climbing expeditions. Rocco ate and fed Sadie with whichever hand she wasn't doctoring. "I ordered some tablecloths from the laundry room. I thought they'd come with the meal, but they're not here yet."

After everyone had a chance to share, the dinner conversation focused on a variety of party-related chatter. Sadie continued to grumble about the tablecloths. Zara knew she really wanted this party to be perfect. They could get them later, but it would help so much with the decorations now.

When the meal was finished, Kestrel volunteered to escort the Littles up to the fifth floor with the decorations. Zara was better about stepping into the elevator, but none of the men would risk her being alone again.

"Hey, do you mind dropping off the ladies and then

taking the cart with our dishes back to the kitchen?" Caesar asked Kestrel.

"On it," Kestrel agreed, wheeling the cart toward the opening doors.

In a flash, they arrived on the top floor. Zara watched Kestrel scan the open area before allowing them to exit. He held Zara back as the others stepped into the gathering room.

"I'll be just a few minutes. Stay with the Littles," he instructed.

"I'll be fine. Stop worrying, Daddy. Magnus is babysitting us," Zara reminded him.

"I'll be right back," he stressed and let her go get ready for tomorrow's party.

Zara shook her head when the doors closed. "I think he worries more about me than I do about myself," she told her friends.

"One thousand percent," Celeste agreed as Sadie nodded.

"I'm going to run and brush my teeth before I blow up balloons," Zara said.

"Oh, that's a good idea," Sadie agreed. "I always feel better with that done."

The three ran into their own apartments to clean their teeth before decorating. Zara forced herself to ignore the boxes in their apartment and was the first one back. She looked at the bare table and smacked her forehead. No one had gotten the tablecloths for the tables. Running back into their apartment for her phone, Zara turned it on to call her Daddy. Something was wrong with it—the screen stayed black.

Crap! It isn't charged.

Her Daddy had accompanied her everywhere. Zara hadn't used her phone for days. She hated for her Daddy to make a trip up and back down again for tablecloths. She knew exactly where they were in the laundry room. It would just take a second.

Hesitating at the elevator door, Zara swallowed hard. Could she get in there by herself? She could take the stairs.

"What's wrong, Zara?" Sadie asked behind her.

"We don't have the tablecloths for the table. I know where they are. Would you run down with me to get them?"

"That's not a good idea. You're not supposed to be in any of the guest areas," Sadie reminded her.

"I know. But you said at dinner that you haven't seen anyone suspicious checking in for a while," Zara reminded her. "Maybe, they've figured out I'm too well-guarded here."

"That's a big risk. We can just wait for a minute, and Kestrel will be back."

"Or we could go get them..."

"Go get what?" Celeste asked.

"Tablecloths. They're just down in the laundry room. That's super close to the elevator," Zara urged. "We need them now to set all the decorations on."

"Magnus will never open the elevator for us," Celeste pointed out. "We'd have to take the stairs."

"They're always deserted. Come on!"

"We're going to get in so much trouble if we get caught," Celeste pointed out.

"Just tell your Daddies that I left and you followed me to make sure I was safe. You're like my bodyguards," Zara suggested.

"Oooh, that helps us but not your bottom," Sadie pointed out.

"We'll have to be fast and get back before anyone notices we're gone," Zara urged, clattering down the stairs with the others on her heels.

"Kestrel, the three Littles headed down the stairwell." Magnus's voice sounded urgent.

"What?" Kestrel barked into the phone from where he stood in the elevator. "Couldn't you stop them? How long ago?"

"Fifteen minutes. I'm sorry, I was on a sweep outside and just got to the interior feeds."

"Push the button for the next floor and take the stairs," Magnus urged.

"We may have a spanking party," Kestrel suggested as he pushed the button. "Better notify the others."

Dashing out of the elevator when it opened, he ran to the stairwell and listened. Silence. They were outside in the resort somewhere.

"One bottom is going to be so red," he muttered as he descended.

Reaching the bottom floor, he tried to decide which way they'd gone. What could they have been after?

Guests milled around the lobby. He dodged between vacationers as he looked over their heads. Kestrel spotted Hawking coming from the elevator.

"Magnus says the laundry room," the large man called to him.

Immediately, Kestrel headed that way, dodging guests. His phone buzzed, and he answered on the run.

"My camera's been knocked out in the laundry room," Magnus reported. "Something is blocking the signal."

Bursting into the large space, he looked around. "No one's here," he told Hawking as he arrived a few steps behind.

At the sound of his voice, a banging started. Following

the sound, he spotted two worried faces in the window of the enormous door on the industrial-sized dryer and ripped it open. "What the fuck!"

Celeste and Sadie talked over each other.

"It's Mark," Sadie shouted.

"He's got Zara," said Celeste.

"He dragged her off that way!" Sadie pointed to the back door.

"I'll get them out. You go. I'll be right behind you," Hawking called out as Kestrel pelted from the room.

"He made us climb in here," Sadie exclaimed.

When his phone buzzed, Kestrel answered, "Magnus, where are they?"

"My cameras are going out sporadically. I'm having trouble watching everywhere," Magnus said softly in his ear. "Rocco's on his way to stay with the other Littles."

Kestrel could hear the frustration and concern in his voice. A thought burst into his mind. "Do the disruptions form a path?"

"Crap! That's it. Head toward the parking lot by the pool!" Magnus ordered.

As Kestrel dashed in that direction, Magnus said, "He must have some kind of blocker that is taking out the cameras along his path. I can't see if he is armed or if there's anyone besides Mark. Back-up is coming, Kestrel. Be careful."

"I'm here. I can't see anything. The parking lot is empty," Kestrel reported before yelling, "Zara?"

"Hey, I'm here," Caesar called out as he joined Kestrel.

"There's no one here. Keep looking, Magnus. There has to be some sign of them."

Phoenix arrived with pounding footsteps. "Where are they?"

"Spread out, and let's check in vehicles," Kestrel ordered.

Methodically, the guys looked into the interior of each car as they called Zara's name. The sun was setting, leaving the area illuminated by lighting but with growing shadows. Finding nothing, they regrouped in the middle of the lot. Caesar's and Phoenix's headshakes told the whole story. No one was stashed in the parking lot.

"This was the only thing I found," Phoenix reported, holding a remote-controlled drone. "It was in its own parking space."

"What is it?" Magnus asked, through the phone connection he still maintained with Kestrel.

When Phoenix shared his discovery, Magnus groaned. "That's how he did it. He created a distraction with a pre-programmed toy. It must be loaded with a device to interfere with the visuals."

"I didn't think I could hate this guy any more. He's literally playing us, and we fell for it," Caesar said with a fiery look.

"Magnus, did any vehicles leave the parking lot after the attack?" Kestrel demanded urgently.

"I've run the footage for the entire resort. There were seven cars, two vans, and a delivery truck that left the resort during the time after the girls ran down the stairs and now. Thank goodness this isn't a heavy traffic time. I'm working on running license plates for all but one dark van that didn't appear to have tags. That one I tracked to the highway."

"Do you still know where that dark van is?" Kestrel asked, thinking it was the likeliest vehicle.

"Yes. It's going into an area that isn't heavily inhabited. Camera coverage will be spotty, and the darkness will challenge any existing footage."

Kestrel took off for the helicopter pad. When his teammates shouted that they would follow by car, Kestrel waved to acknowledge he'd heard them. Within minutes, he had the helicopter prepped and ready to go, but each second felt like a lifetime. Donning his headset, Kestrel disconnected from the phone call and accessed Magnus through the relay.

"I'm going up. Send me the coordinates."

After entering the precise information the computer wizard had shared, Kestrel waited, holding his breath for the location to appear on his screen. The moment it did, he guided the helicopter into the air. The copter covered chunks of miles but wasn't fast enough. He passed over a Danger Bluff SUV driving in the same direction.

"I'm losing it," reported Magnus.

"I'm almost there," Kestrel muttered, leaning forward automatically as if that would help him see farther in the growing darkness.

At the last pinpointed location, he found nothing. Making concentric circles around that area, Kestrel shouted, "I've got it!" After giving the geographic information, he followed the van. He knew Magnus would relay his information to his teammates on the ground.

The van pulled into a packed parking lot, and a single man left the vehicle and walked into a large building, carrying a large bundle over his shoulder. Kestrel circled, looking for a location to set the helicopter down as he shared the information on autopilot. *Fuck!* There was no place to land.

He hovered over the building and focused a spotlight on the sign. *Fuck!*

"What's happening?" Magnus asked quickly.

"This isn't it. It's a rug restoration company. Didn't Sadie call to have the large entrance rug picked up for repair?" Kestrel asked, feeling his hope collapsing as three men walked out to check on the noise of the helicopter hovering over them.

"Let me check."

In a few seconds, Magnus was back on the line. "You're right. They came to pick it up this evening. The guy was running late. You should see the SUV now. Phoenix is almost there."

From above, Kestrel spotted the Danger Bluff vehicle. He focused. It stopped at the front, and both men piled out to run to the door. "Update the guys," he requested, peering through the darkness now that the sun had set completely.

The lights of the helicopter and the parking lot allowed him to see a small bit of the action below. He could have focused the spotlight on them but chose not to due to his growing confidence that this was not Mark. He'd either mixed up the van with another similar one as he'd followed, or this had never been the vehicle that had taken Zara away.

Heading back to Danger Bluff, sick to the core, Kestrel wouldn't sleep until he found her.

Chapter Twenty-Four

Zara struggled against the strips of material around her waist that tied her to the piping on the wall. Her wrists burned from the rubbing of the bonds over her delicate skin as she tried to weaken the fabric to free herself. That asshole Mark had delivered her to the brute who had tethered her here.

How had she not known that he was a bad guy? He'd never said an impolite word or looked at her speculatively or lewdly. In fact, it had seemed that her appearance hadn't made any impact on him. Zara had loved feeling at ease with him.

That worked out well for you, didn't it?

Kicking herself for not detecting Mark's evil plans, she stopped struggling and lowered her head as the two men came into view so she could listen to their conversation. It sounded like this was not the first time Mark had delivered a woman to these men. They berated him for only bringing one tonight until Mark stepped closer to her, grabbed a handful of her hair, and yanked her head back to reveal her face. Instantly, the tone changed.

"Is she a virgin?"

"How would I know? She didn't go out with anyone that I knew about, but those guys at Danger Bluff were very protective. I'm sure one of them was screwing her. I mean, come on..." Mark let his voice trail off to insinuate that she could have been having sex with all six.

"They're going to come after me. You don't want to keep me here," Zara said to them with false bravado.

"You won't be here long, but thanks for the warning," the man with whom Mark had negotiated assured her.

When Mark laughed, her heart sank. It would take the guys time to figure out how Mark had gotten her out of Danger Bluff. If only she'd been able to leave them a clue. The Littles would have told the guys that Mark had abducted her, but that wouldn't get them very far.

Zara breathed out a heavy breath. Thank goodness he had locked them in the dryer instead of hurting them. They hadn't wanted to climb inside, but Mark had held Zara's arm painfully and threatened to break it. Celeste and Sadie had maneuvered their way slowly into the industrial-sized tub, trying to buy as much time as possible. No one had really been sure whether Mark would turn on the dryer or not. At least he hadn't injured her friends.

"They will find me—and both of you. Be smart. Just let me go," Zara said.

"I'll take the risk for a huge reward. Now, shut up, or I'll gag you," the stranger ordered.

Zara looked at Mark, hoping he'd get her silent message. Surely, he wouldn't want to take on the team. Mark shook his and laughed as he turned his back to her. There was no mistaking that he didn't feel an ounce of remorse for endangering her. He pulled out his phone and checked something.

"The money's in my account. Thank you. I'll be in touch when I get to my next employer."

"Who knew the laundry rooms of hotels would be a treasure trove? Where did you find her?" the stranger asked as he walked Mark out of the room.

"We all have to have our secrets," Mark answered.

Zara rested her head against the cold metal of the pipes. She wasn't the first woman Mark had turned over. Who was she kidding? Not turned over. Sold. Mark had sold her. Feeling sick, Zara closed her eyes and hoped with all her energy that Kestrel would be able to find her.

Time drifted by. Locked in the room without windows, Zara had no idea if it had been four hours or a day. Her stomach growled angrily, and she needed to use the restroom.

When she felt like she was going to wet her pants, Zara called out. "Can you hear me? I need to use the toilet."

Silence answered her.

She tried again. "Help! Can anyone hear me?"

Nothing.

Finally, her body lost its battle. Trapped in urine-soaked jeans on the concrete floor, Zara battled despair. Maybe the team had given up on her. Maybe they hadn't even tried to find her. She closed her eyes and allowed her mind to escape into sleep.

"Get up!" A rough hand grabbed her arm and hauled her to her feet.

One foot had fallen asleep in her weird position, and Zara would have fallen if he hadn't stabilized her with an increasingly painful grip.

"Ouch. I'm trying. My foot's asleep." As she tried to balance, she noted that another man had joined them.

"You smell." Her captor frowned at Zara.

Instantly, Zara felt her face heat with embarrassment and knew she was blushing. *How dare he!* "If you'd gotten off your ass and let me use the toilet, I wouldn't smell."

"A bucket of water will solve our problem. Tyler! Get some water to clean Her Majesty," he mocked.

The other man turned without saying a word and left the room. When he returned about five minutes later, the man still held Zara in place on her feet. She wanted to kick him hard but knew that wouldn't free her hands from the pipe. The only result would be him hurting her at least twice as much as she bruised him.

When her captor stepped back, Zara steadied herself on the pipes running the length of the building. As soon as he was clear, his accomplice threw the bucket of water over her.

Zara turned by reflex to deflect the cascade from the front of her body. Icy, cold water hit her back with enough force to push her forward. A gasp escaped from her mouth before she began shivering. The warehouse or wherever they were holding her wasn't heated. The now-drenched clothing made her shiver as the chill seemed to seep into her bones.

"Get another one. We'll do her front, too. The buyers might as well see all her assets," the captor declared.

"No. Please! I'll catch pneumonia," Zara pleaded as his lackey headed back out of the room to follow his orders.

"You won't before I get money for you. Then I don't care what happens to you. Think of it this way, maybe you won't last too long. I know some women beg to die every day. We could be doing you a favor."

With her mind boggled by this statement, tears gathered in Zara's eyes. The slap of another bucket of frigid water against her face and body washed away the last of her hope. He was right. She could see how death was an escape from the horror that awaited.

"But who knows?" he continued. "Maybe your buyer will be a kind, considerate man. Or he could use a bull whip on you until skin can't grow on your back."

Something about this man wanting to scare her fueled her resistance. She could tell he expected her to beg for mercy. Stiffening her spine, she refused to let him see her fear.

"Oh, you still have some fire? Good. That usually raises the price."

The man approached once again. Quickly fastening what looked like a choke leash around her throat, he lifted up and forward, forcing her to move the way he wanted or cut off her oxygen supply. He cut the restraints from her waist, dragged Zara out of the room, and attached her leash to a dangling chain that hung from a beam in the larger room.

Noticing the numerous TV screens, she tried to hide her face while glaring at each man. *I see you. I'm going to make sure you pay.*

"A quarter of a million dollars," bid a voice, harsh with excitement.

"A quarter of a million is paltry for this prize." Her captor grabbed the back of Zara's hair and tugged her face fully up. A fraction of a second passed, and then a new voice with a foreign accent she didn't recognize bid, "Five hundred thousand dollars."

"How many times have you been fucked?" the man demanded, pulling her hair until tears streamed down her face.

"A hundred," she lied.

"See gentlemen? She's barely broken in. By the time you

and your guests are finished with her, she'll know exactly how to please a man."

Shock made her freeze in place. Being raped by one man was bad enough. Her captor thought they would share her with others?

"Let us see her body," one man demanded. "Those wet clothes could hide a myriad of skin diseases and deformities."

"Mr. U, I am known for the integrity of my wares. Would you like to restate that?" her captor bristled.

"This is against the law. You can't just buy and sell me. I have rights," Zara blurted.

"What rights do you have? Let me see your passport. We'll be sure to follow your home country's laws," her captor mocked.

"It's...it's back at Danger Bluff."

"An illegal alien in New Zealand. The laws are very strict here."

"I'll take my chances with the law," Zara stated firmly.

"Seven hundred and fifty thousand dollars," a voice called, and Zara watched one of the images switch to an official law enforcement logo on the wall.

He worked for the very people she hoped would intervene.

Her bravado crashed around her, and Zara covered her face with her hands. She didn't want to see their reaction as the man flipped open a knife and sliced up the back of her shirt. He yanked it down her arms, pulling her hands from her face and exposing her from the waist up.

"One million dollars."

Chapter Twenty-Five

"We should get to have her," the captor's accomplice asserted as he led her back to the room where they'd held Zara first.

"We don't mess with the merchandise," her captor snarled.

Zara could tell the second in command didn't agree with that answer. He shoved her through the doorway and refastened her hands to the pipe. When he tried to cop a feel, Zara squirmed and even tried to bite him.

Immediately, the man drew a hand back to strike her. "Not on the face," the other captor warned from the doorway. "If you drop her value, the difference comes out of your cut, not mine."

The man's palm stopped inches from her face. The gust of wind made her cringe away. "Yeah. Not worth it. She'll be torn and battered in a couple of days. Maybe we can convince them to let us know before they drop her in the ocean."

"The auction will continue for the next three hours. Then, the winner will pick her up within an hour after that."

She had four hours. Maybe not even that long. The guys must not have known where she was. They wouldn't be able to find her before the deal was finalized.

Thank God he'd stayed up in the air, searching the area until his fuel tank had run dangerously low. Heading back to Danger Bluff, he'd risked one last foray in the opposite direction. There, he'd spotted a white van tucked almost completely under the shelter of a lean-to by a decrepit warehouse. Shiny new internet cables reflected his banked lights. Thick bundles of power and connectivity flowed through a window, and there was a glow from lights inside. A funny feeling in the pit of his stomach told him this was not just some homeless encampment. He needed to investigate further.

Not wanting to clue in the men holding Zara, he'd been unwilling to risk hovering over the area in the helicopter. Something flying overhead would've seemed normal enough. A helicopter hovering over the warehouse would've attracted attention. After relaying the coordinates, he'd forced himself to take the helicopter back to Danger Bluff.

"Meet me at the helicopter pad."

The team minus Rocco were all waiting for him by the time he parked. They were dressed in all black. Rocco, already in caretaker mode with the two traumatized Littles, had stayed back at the resort to keep them from harm.

"Here, change as you talk," Caesar ordered, holding out a pair of black pants and a black jacket.

"Magnus has the location pinpointed. It's a hot spot of

communication relays. Something is definitely going on there," Phoenix reported.

"We go in and look around," Kestrel announced as he changed.

"Gathering information is smart. You're going to have trouble not diving into the action," Phoenix warned.

"Worry more that this bucket of bolts won't fall apart on the way," Kestrel warned as he patted a hand on the SUV.

"Phoenix is a wizard with mechanical things. It may look like it belongs in the dump, but this has more power than a sportscar," Caesar said.

Shaking his head, Kestrel climbed into the SUV. The purr of the motor as Phoenix started it told him everything he needed to know. They traversed the darkened streets and arrived at the warehouse.

"Do you need to stay with the vehicle?" Magnus asked.

"That's not going to happen," Kestrel stated firmly.

"Two people in to scout. Wear your comms," Magnus said, handing everyone an earpiece.

"I'm going with you," Hawking said to Kestrel as he fitted his earpiece into place.

"Thanks."

The two men shimmied up a drain pipe and let themselves in through a hole in the roof. From their position above, they were able to see eight guys stationed around the inside of the warehouse and two at the door. Kestrel tensed as he watched a man lead Zara to a large room and bind her in place.

Even though they couldn't hear clearly what was said, there was no mistaking what was happening. When a man moved to strike her, Kestrel lunged forward.

Grabbing a handful of his black jacket, Hawking held Kestrel back until he got control of his anger. Then they lurked in the darkness of the abandoned warehouse. Consumed with hate, Kestrel forced himself to shift his focus to Hawking. The large man shook his head and nodded back the way they'd come. Dragging himself away from the crumpled form of Zara now leaning against the wall, Kestrel led the way back onto the roof and down to the ground.

"Ten guys in the warehouse," Hawking reported, taking the lead while Kestrel pulled himself together.

"And one more at the door and another in the van," Magnus added. "I made a loop around the building, looking for tech. All the power is coming through that window. Unfortunately, those last two guys are virtually standing on top of it."

"We need to take that out so the rescue isn't broadcast all over. Any ideas, Magnus?" Hawking asked.

"Sure. An electronic blocker can stop the transmission from here, but they'll know immediately that a rescue effort is underway," Magnus pointed out.

"So, we take care of the inside guys who are outside the televised room, one by one. Then, we cut it just before we eliminate the guys close to the live feed," Phoenix suggested.

"That's the way to do it," Magnus agreed.

"I'm going inside," Kestrel declared. The others knew there was no way he wasn't going to be in range of Zara.

"Outside," Phoenix chose.

"Inside," Magnus said.

"Inside," Hawking called out.

"Outside," Caesar said last.

They split up and strategized. Kestrel didn't waste time. He asserted his intentions and retraced his steps to the roof. The others followed quickly.

His first target? The man who'd barely restrained himself

from slapping Zara. Finding him from above, Kestrel thought furiously about how to get the jerk away from the area.

"Hey, I'm headed to the john," the man volunteered generously.

After jumping silently down from the rafters, Kestrel beat the fucker to the bathroom and waited just inside. The man never saw it coming. As soon as he stepped into the room, Kestrel took him out with a quick twist of his neck.

Less than a minute passed before Kestrel rejoined Magnus and Hawking.

The two at the door were their next targets. Phoenix and Caesar would come up with some way to eliminate them without alerting those inside. Kestrel trusted his team with his life. Closing his eyes to shake his head, he realized he was also trusting them to save his Little girl.

Sure enough, Kestrel watched as Phoenix and Hawking silently slit the throats of both men at the door simultaneously and with only a whisper of sound.

They moved quickly and efficiently. The man in charge was wrapped up in the bids coming in and didn't notice the quiet until the internet went down. He called for two of his minions to get it back up fast. When no one answered, he drew his knife and headed into the room where Zara sat crumpled against the wall, trying to shield her breasts and face from the camera focused on her.

"No," she shouted as the man appeared. "I won't let this happen."

"Unfortunately, that's out of your control." He sliced through the cloth binding her wrists to the piping and dragged her toward the door.

"Not happening," Kestrel said as he filled the doorway, feeling Magnus's and Hawking's presence behind him.

"I guess you're her big tough boyfriend?" the man

holding her sneered. "Here's your decision. I can slice her throat, letting her bleed out in a few minutes, or you can let both of us walk out of here. Dead is dead. You might find her alive somewhere."

"Neither of those options are going to happen," Kestrel assured him. "You're going to die, and she's going to be free."

"Someone else will just come after her. She's a rare prize." He allowed his knife to prick into the thin skin of her neck.

Kestrel drew in a breath as Phoenix slid down the piping behind the man holding Zara. "Lift your feet, Zara."

He was pleased that she didn't hesitate. Not expecting her weight to shift, the man scraped her skin with the knife as she dropped to the floor. Phoenix eliminated the threat with a quick twist of the trafficker's head. He crumpled to the floor as Kestrel ran forward to scoop Zara into his arms.

"Close your eyes, Little Swan. You don't want to see this," he ordered as he carried her from the building. Bodies were scattered along their path. He counted silently to make sure all the assailants were eliminated.

"Is it over?" she asked in a shaking tone that was difficult to understand.

"It's over."

"Someone else will just come get me," she wailed as Kestrel entered the SUV and held her on his lap. He quickly pulled his black jacket off and wrapped it around her bare torso.

The other men piled in silently, and they were on their way immediately. Kestrel tried to console his Little but knew her beauty risked another attempt to take her.

Distracting himself, he looked around the van at his teammates. "I can't even begin to thank you."

"You could scar me up. Make me ugly. I could do it," Zara offered.

"You are not going to hurt yourself, Little Swan," Kestrel said, squashing that idea.

"So, it turns out that I'm as good at prosthetic disguises as Magnus is at electronics," Caesar volunteered. "It would be very easy to create a disguise that Zara can wear when she wants to leave the protected areas of Danger Bluffs. When she's at home, she can be her natural self."

Even Phoenix, who was driving, twisted in his seat to look at Caesar.

"Hey, I've been thinking about saying something but didn't want to overstep. Prosthetics are a pain to wear. They itch and are hot. It wouldn't take much to change the symmetry of Zara's face. Wearing them once in a while would be bearable."

"Could I wear it when I'm up in the helicopter with Kestrel or going to the store?" Zara asked.

The hope in her voice made Kestrel's heart skip a beat. He couldn't imagine living like this for years, unable to do all the things other people enjoyed and took for granted.

"We're ordering the materials you'll need tomorrow," Kestrel declared. "You'll show me how to put the prosthetic on?" he asked Caesar. "The changes would have to remain the same every time she wore them."

"Of course. I'll contour them to fit only one way," Caesar promised.

"That skill could come in handy for our operations," Magnus commented, tipping up his baseball cap to meet Caesar's eyes directly.

"Definitely," Caesar affirmed.

"Does anyone else have some super power we should know about?" Hawking asked.

"I can tie a cherry stem into a knot in my mouth, too," Caesar volunteered.

"That will come in handy if we need to impress eighteen-year-olds," Phoenix drawled.

The remainder of the trip was spent in sharing quirky talents. Kestrel worried about Zara's emotional well-being in all this silliness after what she'd experienced.

Capturing her chin, he kissed her lightly. "Want them to shut up?"

"No," she said with a vigorous shake of her head before volunteering, "I'm an expert juggler."

"No way. How many things can you juggle?" Magnus asked.

"Six balls," she reported.

"That's amazing," Kestrel commented and hugged her. The team was helping her recover.

Chapter Twenty-Six

"Let's call my Mom and Dad," Zara suggested, bouncing on the barstool where she'd sat for Caesar as he'd transformed her into someone ordinary. Lower cheekbones, contacts to change her eye color, and a smaller chin made an incredible difference. For her body shape, he'd created a belt that wrapped around her waist, eliminating her hour-glass figure. "It's amazing how much just these contact lenses do. They're so much more comfortable than they used to be."

"I'm glad, Little one," Caesar said, smiling. "That small change is remarkable. There are other things we can do, but this is a good start. If her parents are confused, that'll be an incredible sign."

"I'll get it set up." Magnus bent over his computer.

A half hour later, two familiar faces looked at Kestrel and Zara.

"Kestrel? Did something happen to Zara? Why is she not with you?" Zara's father asked quickly.

Laughing, Zara said quickly, "It's me, *Papá*. We've made

a few alterations, using prosthetics, so I don't draw attention to myself."

"That's amazing, Zara. I would not have recognized my own daughter," her mother marveled. "I hate that the world forces you to do this, but I'm excited for you."

"I can't wait to try out my disguise. Thank you for sending me here," Zara said with gratitude in her tone.

"I think that man next to you had a lot to do with making you happy," her father observed.

She gave a sideways glance to her Daddy. "Yes, Kestrel is very important to me. I love him."

"I love your daughter with all my heart," Kestrel assured the older gentleman.

"We will have to meet in person someday," Zara's father said, pinning him in place.

"We'll see how well Zara can tolerate the disguise, and when we're sure it will be safe, we'll come visit," Kestrel promised. "Or you could come here."

"That is a good option," her mother agreed.

"Time to shut down the connection," Magnus announced. As they said their hurried goodbyes, he disconnected from the call.

"It worked!" Zara flew over to Caesar and hugged him tightly.

"It did. Let me take some pictures so we can do this over and over," Caesar said, setting her away from his body.

By the time, he peeled off the rubber pieces attached to her skin, Zara was itchy. She danced in front of him and sighed in relief as he took each section off.

"You made it about an hour. That's not too bad to start," Caesar complimented her.

She sighed. "I'll have to get better."

"Definitely. We'll practice any time you wish."

"Thanks, Caesar," she said, rushing forward to hug him again.

"Thank you, Caesar," Kestrel said, echoing her words.

"Any time."

She turned back toward Magnus to thank him for arranging the call to her parents and found him grinning wide. It was unusual for him, so she cocked her head to the side. "What?"

Magnus grinned wider as Kestrel wrapped an arm around Zara. "I have good news. While you were on the phone, I got a notification that Mark was arrested at the border."

Everyone gasped. Zara was stunned. "Really? Will they be able to do anything about the money he was paid to sell me?"

"Yep. His bank account was frozen. I had already taken care of that. Hopefully the police can trace where the money came from and arrest someone higher up."

Kestrel hugged Zara to his side. "That's really good news."

Celeste skipped into the room and clapped her hands, making them all turn her direction. "Are you guys done with the disguise because it's time for the party!"

Zara glanced at her Daddy, grinning. "Can we go upstairs for the party now, Daddy?" The party had been postponed after Zara had been kidnapped, but it was time to reclaim her life, and Sadie and Celeste agreed that the best way to take control of her life and stop the bad guys from having power over her was to celebrate.

Zara had a lot to celebrate. She'd found the most amazing man as a life partner and her Daddy. She had the best job she could have ever hoped for, working with Celeste. She had great friends and the most beautiful place on earth to explore.

Sure, she had nightmares, but they were starting to occur less frequently, and her Daddy was always there with his arms around her to pull her back into the present.

Zara bounced around excitedly as her Daddy accompanied the girls upstairs to put the finishing touches on their party decorations. When Zara went into her apartment to change into the prettiest party dress she'd ever seen—thanks to her Daddy's amazing taste—she paused in the middle of their apartment and looked around.

Kestrel came up behind her and pulled her back against his front. "You really did turn this boring apartment into a home. Thank you, Little Swan. The colors really brighten the rooms."

"They make me smile," she said as she turned in his arms. "You make me smile, too." She rose on her tiptoes and kissed her Daddy soundly. "I love you."

"I love you too, Little Swan."

"Now, let's get ready to party!"

The next evening, they were all gathered for dinner when Sadie entered the basement holding a small mailing envelope. "Magnus, something was just delivered for you."

"Oooh! It's Magnus's turn," Celeste celebrated.

Magnus didn't like the spotlight. He never wanted to have anyone focused on him. This, however, held special possibilities. Surely, Baldwin Kinglsey III would screw up someone's assignment, and it wouldn't be his Little girl. Taking the package, he tore it open and poured a flash drive and message onto his palm.

Magnus Taverson, your marker has been called into effect. Here is your assignment. Protect Juniper Hazen. The encrypted drive contains all the background information I can provide you.

Baldwin Kingsley III

"Pull it up," Phoenix ordered, earning a glare from the tech guy.

"I don't suppose you'd all get out of here and let me look at it alone...?"

"Not happening," Rocco said with a tickled grin. "You're going to need us at some point. You might as well bring us in from the beginning."

Leaning forward, Magnus opened the drive. A picture of a blonde with green eyes looked back at him. He groaned at the sight of the press nametag hanging around her neck while being drawn to the lonely expression in her eyes.

"This is Juniper Hazen. She's thirty-two and a freelance photographer," Magnus read.

"Thank goodness, she's not a full-time reporter. That could be dangerous," Caesar teased.

"She visited Danger Bluff as a child when it opened originally," Magnus continued.

"What's the threat against her?" Sadie asked.

"None that I can see. She is quirky and has few friends," Magnus read.

"That's sad. Everyone needs friends. Why is she coming to New Zealand?" Zara asked.

"She's on vacation and wants to see what we've done with Danger Bluff...?" Phoenix suggested.

Magnus drew in a breath. "Your guess is as good as mine. She arrives tomorrow."

"So, the team won't have to rescue her?" Rocco asked,

tugging his Little girl to his side. He kissed Sadie's temple softly.

"You never know what Kingsley has in mind for us. There has to be more to the story. I'll do some digging," Magnus promised.

"In the meantime, I'll put her on the fourth floor. She'll be as close to us as possible," Sadie suggested.

"Thank you. Would you let me know when she arrives?" Magnus asked.

"Of course."

As the rest of the team scattered, Magnus continued to stare at the pictures of Juniper Hazen. Her green eyes seemed to bore into him. "What's your story, Little girl?" he murmured to himself.

Rocco, Hawking, and Kestrel had all seemed to feel an instantaneous bond to the women they'd been chosen to protect. As Magnus rubbed his chest, he felt that same instinct. It was uncanny. How could Kingsley possibly have that kind of power?

Magnus wasn't the sort of man who smiled very often, but as he stared at Juniper, he felt the corners of his mouth lifting. Whatever she was facing, he would be right next to her battling her demons.

Authors' Note

We hope you're enjoying Danger Bluff! Each of the men you've met in this series will get their own happily ever after. Stay tuned for all six books coming soon!

Danger Bluff:
Rocco

Hawking

Kestrel

Magnus

Phoenix

Caesar

About Becca Jameson

Becca Jameson is a USA Today best-selling author of over 140 books. She is well-known for her Wolf Masters series, her Fight Club series, and her Surrender series. She currently lives in Houston, Texas, with her husband. Two grown kids pop in every once in a while too! She is loving this journey and has dabbled in a variety of genres, including paranormal, sports romance, military, reverse harem, dark romance, suspense, dystopian, and BDSM.

A total night owl, Becca writes late at night, sequestering herself in her office with a glass of red wine and a bar of dark chocolate, her fingers flying across the keyboard as her characters weave their own stories.

During the day--which never starts before ten in the morning!--she can be found walking, running errands, or reading in her favorite hammock chair!

...where Alphas dominate...

Becca's Newsletter Sign-up

Join my Facebook fan group, Becca's Bibliomaniacs, for the most up-to-date information, random excerpts while I work, giveaways, and fun release parties!

Facebook Fan Group:
Becca's Bibliomaniacs

Contact Becca:
www.beccajameson.com
beccajameson4@aol.com

facebook.com/becca.jameson.18
x.com/beccajameson
instagram.com/becca.jameson
bookbub.com/authors/becca-jameson
goodreads.com/beccajameson
amazon.com/author/beccajameson

Also by Becca Jameson

Seattle Doms:

Salacious Exposure

Salacious Desires By Kate Oliver

Salacious Attraction

Salacious Devotion

Danger Bluff:

Rocco

Hawking

Kestrel

Magnus

Phoenix

Caesar

Roses and Thorns:

Marigold

Oleander

Jasmine

Tulip

Daffodil

Lily

Bite of Pain Anthology: Gemma's Release

Shadowridge Guardians:

Steele by Pepper North

Kade by Kate Oliver

Atlas by Becca Jameson

Doc by Kate Oliver

Gabriel by Becca Jameson

Talon by Pepper North

Blossom Ridge:

Starting Over

Finding Peace

Building Trust

Feeling Brave

Embracing Joy

Accepting Love

Blossom Ridge Box Set One

Blossom Ridge Box Set Two

The Wanderers:

Sanctuary

Refuge

Harbor

Shelter

Hideout

Haven

The Wanderers Box Set One

The Wanderers Box Set Two

Surrender:

Raising Lucy

Teaching Abby

Leaving Roman

Choosing Kellen

Pleasing Josie

Honoring Hudson

Nurturing Britney

Charming Colton

Convincing Leah

Rewarding Avery

Impressing Brett

Guiding Cassandra

Surrender Box Set One

Surrender Box Set Two

Surrender Box Set Three

Open Skies:

Layover

Redeye

Nonstop

Standby

Takeoff

Jetway

Open Skies Box Set One

Open Skies Box Set Two

Shadow SEALs:

Shadow in the Desert

Shadow in the Darkness

Holt Agency:

Rescued by Becca Jameson

Unchained by KaLyn Cooper

Protected by Becca Jameson

Liberated by KaLyn Cooper

Defended by Becca Jameson

Unrestrained by KaLyn Cooper

Delta Team Three (Special Forces: Operation Alpha):

Destiny's Delta

Canyon Springs:

Caleb's Mate

Hunter's Mate

Corked and Tapped:

Volume One: Friday Night

Volume Two: Company Party

Volume Three: The Holidays

Project DEEP:

Reviving Emily

Reviving Trish

Reviving Dade

Reviving Zeke

Reviving Graham

Reviving Bianca

Reviving Olivia

Project DEEP Box Set One

Project DEEP Box Set Two

SEALs in Paradise:

Hot SEAL, Red Wine

Hot SEAL, Australian Nights

Hot SEAL, Cold Feet

Hot SEAL, April's Fool

Hot SEAL, Brown-Eyed Girl

Dark Falls:

Dark Nightmares

Club Zodiac:

Training Sasha

Obeying Rowen

Collaring Brooke

Mastering Rayne

Trusting Aaron

Claiming London

Sharing Charlotte

Taming Rex

Tempting Elizabeth

Club Zodiac Box Set One

Club Zodiac Box Set Two

Club Zodiac Box Set Three

The Art of Kink:

Pose

Paint

Sculpt

Arcadian Bears:

Grizzly Mountain

Grizzly Beginning

Grizzly Secret

Grizzly Promise

Grizzly Survival

Grizzly Perfection

Arcadian Bears Box Set One

Arcadian Bears Box Set Two

Sleeper SEALs:

Saving Zola

Spring Training:

Catching Zia

Catching Lily

Catching Ava

Spring Training Box Set

The Underground series:

Force

Clinch

Guard

Submit

Thrust

Torque

The Underground Box Set One

The Underground Box Set Two

Wolf Masters series:

Kara's Wolves

Lindsey's Wolves

Jessica's Wolves

Alyssa's Wolves

Tessa's Wolf

Rebecca's Wolves

Melinda's Wolves

Laurie's Wolves

Amanda's Wolves

Sharon's Wolves

Wolf Masters Box Set One

Wolf Masters Box Set Two

Claiming Her series:

The Rules

The Game

The Prize

Claiming Her Box Set

Emergence series:

Bound to be Taken

Bound to be Tamed

Bound to be Tested

Bound to be Tempted

Emergence Box Set

The Fight Club series:

Come

Perv

Need

Hers

Want

Lust

The Fight Club Box Set One

The Fight Club Box Set Two

Wolf Gatherings series:

Tarnished

Dominated

Completed

Redeemed

Abandoned

Betrayed

Wolf Gatherings Box Set One

Wolf Gathering Box Set Two

Durham Wolves series:

Rescue in the Smokies

Fire in the Smokies

Freedom in the Smokies

Durham Wolves Box Set

Stand Alone Books:

Blind with Love

Guarding the Truth

Out of the Smoke

Abducting His Mate

Wolf Trinity

Frostbitten

A Princess for Cale/A Princess for Cain

Severed Dreams

Where Alphas Dominate

About Pepper North

Ever just gone for it? That's what *USA Today* Bestselling Author Pepper North did in 2017 when she posted a book for sale on Amazon without telling anyone. Thanks to her amazing fans, the support of the writing community, Mr. North, and a killer schedule, she has now written more than 80 books!

Enjoy contemporary, paranormal, dark, and erotic romances that are both sweet and steamy? Pepper will convert you into one of her loyal readers. What's coming in the future? A Daddypalooza!

Sign up for Pepper North's newsletter

Like Pepper North on Facebook

Join Pepper's Readers' Group for insider information and giveaways!

Follow Pepper everywhere!
Amazon Author Page
BookBub
FaceBook
GoodReads
Instagram
TikToc
Twitter
YouTube
Visit Pepper's website for a current checklist of books!

amazon.com/author/pepper_north

bookbub.com/profile/pepper-north

facebook.com/AuthorPepperNorth

instagram.com/4peppernorth

pinterest.com/4peppernorth

x.com/@4peppernorth

Also By Pepper North

Don't miss future sweet and steamy Daddy stories by Pepper North? Subscribe to my newsletter!

Shadowridge Guardians

Combining the sizzling talents of bestselling authors Pepper North, Kate Oliver, and Becca Jameson, the Shadowridge Guardians are guaranteed to give you a thrill and leave you dreaming of your own throbbing motorcycle joyride.

Are you daring enough to ride with a club of rough, growly, commanding men? The protective Daddies of the Shadowridge Guardians Motorcycle Club will stop at nothing to ensure the safety and protection of everything that belongs to them: their Littles, their club, and their town. Throw in some sassy, naughty, mischievous women who won't hesitate to serve their fair share of attitude even in the face of looming danger, and this brand new MC Romance series is ready to ignite!

Available on Amazon

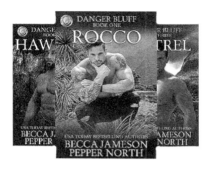

Danger Bluff

Welcome to Danger Bluff where a mysterious billionaire brings together a hand-selected team of men at an abandoned resort in New Zealand. They each owe him a marker. And they all have something in common–a dominant shared code to nurture and protect. They will repay their debts one by one, finding love along the way.

Available on Amazon

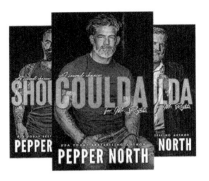

A Second Chance For Mr. Right

For some, there is a second chance at having Mr. Right. Coulda, Shoulda, Woulda explores a world of connections that can't exist... until they do. Forbidden love abounds when these Daddy Doms refuse to live with regret and claim the women who own their hearts.

Available on Amazon

Little Cakes

Welcome to Little Cakes, the bakery that plays Daddy matchmaker! Little Cakes is a sweet and satisfying series, but dare to taste only if you like delicious Daddies, luscious Littles, and guaranteed happily-ever-afters.

Available on Amazon

Dr. Richards' Littles®

A beloved age play series that features Littles who find their forever Daddies and Mommies. Dr. Richards guides and supports their efforts to keep their Littles happy and healthy.

Available on Amazon

Note: Zoey; Dr. Richards' Littles® 1 is available FREE on Pepper's website:

4PepperNorth.club

Dr. Richards' Littles®

is a registered trademark of

With A Wink Publishing, LLC.

All rights reserved.

SANCTUM

Pepper North introduces you to an age play community that is isolated from the surrounding world. Here Littles can be Little, and Daddies can care for their Littles and keep them protected from the outside world.

Available on Amazon

Soldier Daddies

What private mission are these elite soldiers undertaking? They're all searching for their perfect Little girl.

Available on Amazon

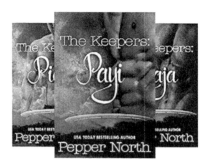

The Keepers

This series from Pepper North is a twist on contemporary age play romances. Here are the stories of humans cared for by specially selected Keepers of an alien race. These are science fiction novels that age play readers will love!

Available on Amazon

The Magic of Twelve

The Magic of Twelve features the stories of twelve women transported on their 22nd birthday to a new life as the droblin (cherished Little one) of a Sorcerer of Bairn. These magic wielders have waited a long time to take complete care of their droblin's needs. They will protect their precious one to their last drop of magic from a growing menace. Each novel is a complete story.

Available on Amazon

Printed in Great Britain
by Amazon

37946086R00136